GW00370817

A SCHOLARLY APPLICATION

Society blue-stocking Lilith Fitzgilbert is the last person anyone would expect to create a scandal. Maverick antiquarian Edward Makepeace is the last person anyone would expect to take on a female scholar. When Lilith perforce retires from London for a month to join Edward's excavation of the Devil's Ditch near Newmarket, neither of them expects to find a run-down house and a dead butler. Nor, on top of everything else, do they expect to fall in love . . .

JAN JONES

A SCHOLARLY APPLICATION

Complete and Unabridged

LINFORD
Leicester

First published in Great Britain in 2019

First Linford Edition
published 2020

A catalogue record for this book is available
from the British Library.

ISBN 978–1–4448–4573–0

Published by
Ulverscroft Limited
Anstey, Leicestershire

Set by Words & Graphics Ltd.
Anstey, Leicestershire
Printed and bound in Great Britain by
T. J. International Ltd., Padstow, Cornwall

This book is printed on acid-free paper

A Scholarly Application
is dedicated to all the misfits
People who refuse to conform

Dramatis Personae

Lilith Fitzgilbert — an independently-minded blue-stocking
[Previously in *A Rational Proposal*]
Benedict Fitzgilbert — Lilith's brother, head of the Pool
[Previously in *A Rational Proposal*]
Hester — Lilith's maid, inherited from her mother
Verity Bowman — Lilith's friend
[Previously in *A Rational Proposal, A Respectable House*]
Julia Congreve — Lilith's friend
[Previously in *A Rational Proposal*]
Woods — Lilith's senior footman
Edward (Ned) Makepeace — A maverick antiquarian
Richard Makepeace — Ned's younger brother
Patterson — Ned's disrespectful town butler

Atkins — Ned's unsatisfactory country butler

Donald Kerr — Ned's secretary

Ferris — Ned's long-suffering valet

Chilcott — Ned's groom

Peter Swann — Ned's new footman

Mrs Bell — Ned's appalling cook

The Duke and Duchess of Rutland — the local nobility

Sir Mortimer Vale — an annoying dilettante

Mr Thornley — Ned's fellow antiquarian with an eye for the ladies

Catherine Redding (aka Kitty Eastwick) — Verity's half-sister, housekeeper at Furze House
[Previously in *A Rational Proposal, A Respectable House*]

Nicholas Dacre — member of the Pool, 'Guvnor' at Furze House
[Previously in *A Rational Proposal, A Respectable House*]

Molly Turner — Catherine's friend, seamstress, occasional lady of the night
[Previously in *A Rational Proposal, A*

Respectable House]

Ma Turner — Molly's mother, laundress

[Previously in *A Respectable House*]

Mrs Smith — Furze House resident with a noisy newborn

Fred Grimes — former hackney driver

[Previously in *A Rational Proposal, A Respectable House*]

John and Selina Bowman — Catherine's brother and sister-in-law

[Previously in *A Rational Proposal, A Respectable House*]

Locke — Ned's retired butler

Various scholars, servants, grooms, boarders, dinner guests and children

Other characters in the *Furze House Irregulars* series

Charles Congreve — Verity's betrothed, Julia's brother, attorney, member of the Pool

[*An Unconventional Act, A Rational Proposal*]

Adam Prettyman — landowner and

former actor, member of the Pool
[*An Unconventional Act, A Rational Proposal, A Respectable House*]
Jenny Prettyman — Adam's wife
[*An Unconventional Act, A Rational Proposal, A Respectable House*]
Lord Alexander Rothwell — politician, member of the Pool
[*A Respectable House*]
Lady Fitz — Lilith and Ben's determinedly artistic stepmama
[*A Rational Proposal*]

Oh, and

Flint — don't ask. Keep your head down. Safer not to know.

Author's Note

A *Scholarly Application* is the third of the Furze House Irregulars books and begins shortly after the events in *A Rational Proposal* and *A Respectable House*. You do not have to have read either of the previous titles to enjoy this story, though naturally I'd be delighted if you bought them as well!

A Rational Proposal introduced Verity Bowman and Charles Congreve. In *A Respectable House*, it was the turn of Verity's half-sister Kitty Eastwick and Charles's friend Nicholas Dacre. Now with *A Scholarly Application*, Verity's friend Lilith Fitzgilbert steps forward, having embroiled herself in a scandal, thus making it necessary to retreat to maverick antiquarian Edward Makepeace's ancient earthwork site in Cambridgeshire until she can return to society.

The fourth (and final) book in the series will be *A Practical Arrangement*, which is Charles's sister Julia Congreve's story.

1

London, November 1817

The Honourable Lilith Fitzgilbert had been to Somerset House many times. She had attended concerts and exhibitions in its chilly stone rooms. She had listened to lectures given by the Royal Society and the Society of Antiquaries (including a fascinating one just last week on discoveries made whilst excavating Egyptian ruins). She had sketched classical statues and studied the portraiture of the leading artists of the past fifty years. Today would be no different. No different at all. She simply had to remember she wasn't wearing skirts.

Lilith pulled her cap lower over her forehead, hoping the Dutch drawing student she'd borrowed it from was correct in saying artisan headgear needn't be removed in the rooms. It was, she reflected, one of the few times any of her stepmama's protégés had actually been useful. Her sketchbook was tucked under her arm. Her pencils were in one pocket of her well-worn coat (also borrowed from Johann, albeit neither garment with his knowledge), one of her brother's handkerchiefs in another. She felt laden down. How did men manage on a daily basis without reticules?

She walked though the vaulted arch and turned right into the Royal Academy. Crossing the chequered vestibule floor, she had a moment's regret that the Life Drawing rooms were not upstairs. She would have liked the freedom of being able to ascend the grand staircase without the hazard of tripping over her hem on the steps. More than once had she seen an unfortunate lady suffer the disaster of not catching her skirts up while ascending, or come to grief descending due to someone being impolitely close on her heels.

With Johann's token as a bona fide student of the Royal Academy gripped in her hand (he really was appallingly lax about his belongings), Lilith joined the queue to gain entrance to the life-drawing demonstration. She kept her head down, as much to hide her recurrent annoyance that these classes were only open to gentlemen as to keep her face in shadow. As the line moved forward, she fortified herself with the thought that these 'Stranger Days', when a leading artist visited the Royal Academy to give a demonstration to all comers, were so rare that when one had coincided with the exact week Johann was away visiting a possible patron (having first requested with a melting smile that his everyday suit was laundered by the maids in the interim), the opportunity to use it must not only be grasped, it must have been *meant*.

The model was already in position on the dais in the centre of the room. The great lamp in the ceiling had been lit, and the reflector deployed so as to direct a powerful beam on the semi-recumbent figure. From where she was perched on the end of a bench, Lilith could only see his right side, but she felt satisfaction flow through her as she took in the sweep of his naked arm and the muscles of his right leg. Drawing classical statues was all very well, but there was no feeling of life to them. It was necessary to know how the body moved beneath the clothes in order to draw people fully dressed.

At the front, the regular students were already at work. Without waiting another moment, Lilith opened her sketchbook, balanced it on her lap and began sketching as fast as she could.

She drew with total concentration, trying to catch the muscles of the model's thigh. The air grew stuffy, the aroma of gentlemen en masse being somewhat overwhelming. It was, how-ever, better than the sudden, unwelcome, too-sweet scent of violets drifting across from behind her left

4

shoulder. Lilith hunched over her drawing. That scent could only be Sir Mortimer Vale. Why was he here? To be seen, presumably. He liked to think of himself as cultured, and he certainly haunted her stepmother's soirées with annoying regularity, but his own drawing was indifferent in the extreme. He did like the association with artists, though. And, Lilith remembered uneasily, he had spent a good portion of time talking to Johann at the last soirée just ten days ago.

'Nice sketch,' said the unctuous voice behind her. He was leaning so closely over her shoulder that under the violets, she could smell the ham and mustard he had partaken of for breakfast.

'*Bedankt*,' she muttered in as deep a voice as she could manage. *Now go away, you wretched man. I'm busy.*

Fortunately, Sir Thomas Lawrence began his lecture then. Lilith, furious with Sir Mortimer for spoiling it for her, slid even closer to the end of the bench, noting the press of gentlemen

5

standing between her and the door and mentally plotting a route between them should it become necessary.

Sir Thomas Lawrence, justly famed for his portraits, was clearly no stranger to the naked form and, like one of Lilith's previous tutors, held the view that true artistic proficiency could only come with regular practice, drawing from life.

In Lilith's case, Mr Foxton had ingeniously proposed his own self as a model to solve the awkwardness inherent in her being a minor and thus ineligible to join his special classes for married women. This offer had been unhappily misunderstood by Papa and had been the cause of considerable friction between him and Lilith's stepmama, it being she who had suggested the tutor from within her circle of artistic acquaintances. Lilith had not even been able to re-engage the man after Papa died. Mr Foxton had been so discomposed by being run out of Bedford Square in a state of nature that he now lived in an artistic colony in Wales, where his progressive views were properly appreciated and his Byronic looks much admired.

Lilith drew and listened, only stretching her cramped fingers when Sir Thomas directed the model to change position and assume an athletic stance facing away from the audience in the three-quarter position. The level of interest in the room rose. Lilith hurriedly turned to a fresh page. A standing figure was an opportunity not to be missed. She had nearly got the whole of his back delineated when she smelled the sickly waft of violets again and felt a hand grasping her arm. Sir Mortimer had climbed down a tier over the semi-circular bench and was exchanging his seat for that of the gentleman next to her, much to the annoyance of the rest of the row.

'You'll never see anything from there, young fellow. Don't be shy, I'll find you a seat on the other side. Much better view.'

Sir Mortimer's voice was oddly thick. Lilith shook him off, annoyed with him for interrupting her. 'Iss goed,' she growled.

His lewd chuckle sent a shudder of revulsion through her. 'I'll wager I know why you're keeping your drawing low. Splendidly developed, isn't he?'

Before she could divine his intention, Sir Mortimer thrust his hand under her sketchbook and seized her between the legs. She gasped in shock.

She wasn't, however, as shocked as Sir Mortimer. He pulled back as if she'd burned him and a second later grabbed at her cap. 'What the devil . . . ?'

Exclamations sounded around them as her hair, pinned up by her friend Julia Congreve to look like a youth's bob, was revealed. Lilith didn't hesitate. Snatching back the cap and cramming the sketchbook under her arm, she slid frantically between all the gentlemen who had arrived late and pelted for the vestibule and the outside world.

2

'You did *what*?' Benedict stared at her in consternation. 'Lilith, this is appalling! It'll be a deuce of a thing to untangle. Whatever possessed you?'

Lilith watched her brother pace the room. She attempted to recapture the righteousness that had filled her this morning. She could see why Ben would be aggrieved. Her brother had a name and a position to keep up, not to mention various secret dealings that needed to remain strictly private. He really didn't want the scandal that was doubtless as hot on her heels as the enraged gentlemen who had dashed after her as she ran from Somerset House to the safety of the small shops along the Strand, where her friends Julia and Verity had been waiting with concealing clothes.

She'd intended confessing as soon as

she returned, but Benedict had been out himself. Now she smoothed the newspaper he'd dropped and said, 'Such a fuss. People are only people, whether clothed or unclothed. I did it partly because I am furious with the Royal Academy for not allowing ladies to attend their classes.'

Ben stopped pacing and turned, puzzlement crossing his face. 'Do you wish to? Two hours' instruction every evening would interfere considerably with your social engagements.'

'No, that would be excessive. But I did want to attend Sir Thomas Lawrence's life-drawing lecture and was not allowed to because I am female.'

She thought he blenched, but he passed it off as a joke. 'Quite right. Ladies observing the naked male body? Whatever next!'

'Next might be that my sketches of gentlemen improve.' She shot a look at her brother. 'I *am* sorry, Ben, really. I did not mean to cause a scandal. I am feeling contrary and I don't know why. The Royal Academy's patronising attitude was suddenly not to be borne. I daresay my crotchets are due to not having a purpose. If I had been able to follow you to Cambridge, I should now be settled in a scholarly way of life which would suit me admirably. As it is, Verity is having adventures and being kidnapped. Her sister had to flee for her life to Newmarket. Even Julia is asking useful gossipy questions for you amongst her society friends. Meanwhile I am twenty-four, unwed, still on the same round of activities as when I was seventeen, and I am bored.'

Her brother crossed the room and took her hand. 'Lilith, my dear, what is this? Do you *want* to be married? Should I stop rejecting the impecunious artists and poets who keep falling violently in love with you? I thought you were content as we are.'

She sighed. 'So I am, in general. Ignore me, Ben; I am talking nonsense. I have never yet met a gentleman who

11

prized my mind above my money, so I certainly do not wish to be married just for the sake of it. It must be seeing Verity and Charles so very much in love. It is unsettling.'

She fixed her gaze on the *Morning Post*, hoping Ben wouldn't notice the unaccustomed tears in her eyes. It was too feeble of her. The morning's adventure had left her more over-wrought than she had expected.

Ben's voice was rueful. 'Well, the result of today's adventure is that you must retire from society for a while. You will not wish to keep to the house, I suppose, so it had better be one of the estates. Which takes your fancy? We have neither of us visited Norfolk for some time.'

'*Norfolk?* In November? The case is hardly that desperate.' Lilith glanced at him speculatively. 'We could go abroad? Rome, perhaps, or Florence? I should like to do something cultural.'

'I cannot go abroad,' replied her brother. 'You know I cannot. The Pool needs me. Flint has become too dangerous.'

The Pool, the loose 'pool of talent' her brother had assembled to combat London's crime. And Flint, the mysterious shadowmaster responsible for a large part of that crime.

Benedict continued, 'We are the only ones with a hope of tracking him. Bow Street doesn't have the resources, so Sir Nathaniel Conant is depending on me to produce some sort of miracle. No, the question as I see it is how we are to come up with a reason why I am *not* whisking you away to the continent until the scandal dies down. How many people actually saw you at Somerset House?'

'Close enough to name me? Apart from Sir Mortimer Vale, not that many. It was too crowded for most of them, and I was near the door. As soon as the wretched man put his hand so familiarly on my . . . on my . . . under my sketchbook, I started moving. When he pulled off Johann's cap and realised it

13

was me, I grabbed it back, pushed through to the door and ran out to the Strand, where Julia and Verity were waiting.'

Benedict knit his brows, his gaze unfocused. 'We may brush through, then. He will not accuse you directly, for it will expose him as well as you.'

Lilith began to feel more encouraged. 'I must say, I had never before appreciated just how convenient a gentleman's attire is for freedom of movement. I covered the distance in no time. Julia had my bonnet in a bandbox and Verity wrapped a cloak around me as soon as I reached them. It was done very fast. We were inside the shop in a trice.'

'You are fortunate in your friends,' said her brother drily. 'It is a pity neither of them thought to dissuade you from the escapade at the outset.'

'I don't believe it entered their heads for a moment,' said Lilith. 'They have previously thought me a pattern card of respectability. You must understand this is the sort of scheme that is meat and drink to Verity. As for Julia, nothing pleases her better than to while away a couple of hours in a parade of shops. She had already decided exactly the bonnet to try on as soon as we whisked inside Mme Dupont's shop. A pale blue Angouleme. It suited her divinely. The only thing any gentlemen would have seen looking through the window was her lovely face turned towards the glass so as to catch the light.'

There was a short silence. Lilith picked up the *Morning Post*. Her maid Hester bustled in, absorbed the atmosphere, and took herself off again.

Benedict cleared his throat. 'Aunt Augusta is still in Holland, if you wish for continental travel.'

Lilith narrowed her eyes at him. 'I understand you are upset, Ben, but there's no need to be vindictive.' She turned a page in the newspaper and her heart thumped. 'Oh! Edward Makepeace is to excavate part of the Devil's Ditch.'

Her brother looked across sharply. 'Makepeace? The antiquarian who writes in the *Gentleman's Magazine?* His name has come up in connection with something else recently. How do you know of him?'

It was meant. Everything fitted. It *had* to be meant. 'I went to a lecture at Somerset House given by Mr Makepeace just last week. Egyptian ruins. I told you. It was remarkably good. He cares about his subject and is an engaging speaker, not to mention answering my question as if I were a person with a mind of my own, rather than an empty-headed female.' She read on. 'He is raising funds for an excavation in Greece next year — which I knew, for he mentioned it during the lecture — but meanwhile is continuing an investigation into an ancient feature on his own land called the Devil's Ditch, which he believes shows East Anglian earthworks were designed and used for barricades during Anglo-Saxon skirmishes. Ben, the Devil's Ditch is near Newmarket! I can go to Furze House to plan the refurbishment which you all say is necessary, and visit the Devil's Ditch during the day to learn about the excavation. Mr Makepeace will surely be happy to take paying pupils if he is raising funds, don't you think?'

'I daresay, but . . . '

'Think, Ben. Verity's sister is at Furze House as housekeeper. I will be out of London long enough for any scandal to die down, which is what you want, and it is not so far that you will be unable to visit me — especially when you need to have secret meetings with the Pool. Should you dislike escorting me there? I will be occupied and I will be learning something new, which is all I ever ask.' *And above all, it is different to the same endless circle of visits and dinners and soirées here.*

Benedict picked up the newspaper and read the article. 'It would serve,' he said slowly. 'If I am to take you, it will have to be on Saturday. I own I should like to see Furze House, as I am funding it.'

There was a hesitation in his voice. 'What is it?' she asked.

He ran a hand through his ordered locks. If nothing else, this showed his sister something was indeed exercising his mind. 'I told you Makepeace's name had come up. Lilith, you know the difficulty the Pool is having trying to track Flint?'

'Yes, and I am pleased that you have at last taken me into your confidence about it.'

'Small chance of keeping you out once your friends were aware of our existence.'

Lilith ignored his sour tone. 'Even without Verity's genius for discovering interesting situations, it was bound to happen. I am not unobservant, Ben.'

'Yes, well . . . when Nicholas Dacre returned from Newmarket last week, he brought evidence that Flint has his talons into far more society gentlemen than we had previously thought. We had

already identified several clubs and
. . . and other houses where the
clientele are vulnerable. Makepeace's
name is on a list regarding one of those
houses. I do not believe him to be
dangerous, or I would not let you go,
but he might be susceptible to pressure
from Flint.'

Lilith's first instinct was one of
outright rejection that Edward Makepeace was involved with anything
shadowy. The strength of her feeling
— on just one lecture and an intelligent
answer to her question — startled her
so much that for a moment she didn't
follow what Benedict was asking. Then
she stared at her brother in astonish-
ment. He was allowing her to help with
his covert work? 'You wish me to report
back?' she asked.

'No, Lilith, I wish you were far away
from any potential intrigue. However,
as you are known to be interested in
antiquities, you have — regrettably — a
reason to retire to the country. It seems
meant.'

Exactly what she had thought, but for a different reason.

'You will be accompanied by your maid, obviously. You will oblige me by taking a footman as well.'

'Certainly. Woods would be a useful addition to Furze House while we are there, and it would be difficult not to take Hester in any case. You will be delighted to hear she has already rung a peal over my head. I daresay she will continue to do so for the next dozen years. However, if we are to leave in two days' time, packing will distract her nicely. I shall inform her directly, and meanwhile I had better order a quiet dinner at home for us tonight.'

'That sounds very soothing. Unfortunately, there is a concert afterwards where I am supposed to meet a gentleman about infiltrations into the military.' Irritation crossed his face. 'And next week we are promised to Lady Huntley's ball. Really, Lilith, this is too bad of you. How am I to manage without you to head off all the insipid lovelies who will make a dead set at me? Who will guard me for the next few weeks from the trophy-hunting mamas and their simpering daughters, eager to add a baron to the family? Who in heaven's name is going to act as my hostess for the formal dinners? Do not suggest our stepmother, I beg of you.'

Lilith shuddered at the very thought. 'You may have to put off the dinners. For other occasions, you need a human cloak. It is a pity you have always refused to countenance the idea of marriage. It is sheer laziness on your part, as I have pointed out before. Is there really no one you wish to wed? A betrothal would instantly put you out of bounds.'

'No one.'

'A sham engagement, then? A practical solution to your difficulties?'

He gave her an ironic look. 'Oh yes, why did I not think of that? That will not be in the least suspicious. I am forever entering into engagements and then breaking them.'

She swatted his arm affectionately. 'Just because you never have before, it does not mean you cannot begin.' *Simply making the time to converse with an unattached lady would be a start*, she thought.

'Oh, and I imagine you will easily find me a lady who needs a short-term arrangement for the winter before she goes back to breeding pugs, or whatever it is she really wants from her life.'

Lilith looked at him thoughtfully. 'She must not be a fright, or it would not be credible.'

'That is immaterial. She must not be a fright because it would be too cruel on her when we parted. I will not make anyone a laughing stock. Lilith, you are not serious? I am not so selfish as to enter into a masquerade purely for my own convenience. It would be monstrous, using a lady for such a reason.'

'Not necessarily. What do you say to Julia Congreve? It would be a significant cachet for her if she was thought to have attracted you.'

Benedict raised his eyebrows in disbelief. 'The friend who makes no move to stop you ruining yourself and putting us in this situation in the first place? I thank you, no.'

'Consider for a moment, Ben. She is interested in all things political, but has little money to do anything about it. That will ensure you always have something to discuss that will not come across as forced in company. The Congreves are a good family. Julia is a friend of mine and moves in our set, so it will not be thought remarkable if you begin to pay her more attention while I am away. You will find her amusing, as she always knows everything about people. More to the point, brother dear, she knows about the Pool.' *And she is beautiful. And perceptive, though she conceals it. A perfect foil for you.*

'It is out of the question. The family is too decent. It would hurt her reputation when we break the engage-ment.'

'Yours, perhaps, not hers. And you do

not have to go so far as an engagement.'

'No, Lilith.'

'We could ask her . . . '

Benedict made the sound of pure male frustration that meant he was giving in.

Lilith hid a smile. 'I will send her a note. Meanwhile, you had best write to Edward Makepeace.'

★   ★   ★

In her mind, Lilith was quite sure Mr Makepeace would accede to her request. After fending off her stepmother's protégés and her aunt's impecunious discoveries for years, she knew to a nicety how quickly a starving artist's moral compass swung to gold when material relief was offered. It did not seem to her that an antiquarian looking to fund an overseas expedition would be any different. After dinner, she therefore set about assembling all she would need for a month's stay in the country.

'Books,' she mused aloud. Leaving

Hester to fold the four evening gowns she was unlikely to require in tissue paper, she went down to the library to select a dozen volumes to keep her amused for the first couple of weeks. She could always write to Benedict to bring her some more.

As she crossed the hall, she intercepted Woods with a letter for her brother.

'From Mr Makepeace,' said the footman.

Lilith smiled. 'Thank you, Woods. I will put it in his study.' Once inside the door, she turned the note over thoughtfully. The single sheet was addressed in a bold hand, carelessly folded and, interestingly, the seal was imperfectly affixed. It was the work of a moment to peel the wax away.

'*No females. This is not a house party,*' she read aloud. There was nothing more. Just that one line and an arrogant scrawl of a signature. How extraordinarily rude.

'Woods,' she said, emerging from the

study again. 'Engage a hackney, will you? I think that will be more discreet than one of our carriages. And then be ready to accompany me to Mr Makepeace's house.' She ran up the stairs. 'Hester! Outdoor shoes, please. We are paying a visit. Yes, I do know what the time is.'

★   ★   ★

If Lilith had ever envisaged an antiquarian's study, this would have been it. The floor was littered with piles of paper and half-full crates. Drifts of wood shavings from those crates suggested the housemaid would shortly be tendering her notice. Folios were piled on most of the available tables. The antiquarian himself, in shirtsleeves, loosened neckcloth, and with his thick fair hair disordered, was rummaging through a drawer which he had hauled out and balanced on top of quite four inches of assorted documents. All in all, the scene was most encouraging.

'Good evening,' she said on being shown into the room and deducing that there was no Mrs Makepeace on the premises or she would have been directed to the salon instead. 'How very nice to meet you again. Your lecture on the Egyptian ruins last week was fascinating. It is rare to find a speaker who takes the trouble to address the whole room rather than just the gentlemen present. Do pray forgive my intrusion. I thought I had better come myself, as you don't seem to have quite understood my brother's letter.'

Edward Makepeace, his hands still turning over the contents of the drawer, raised his head and stared at her in stupefaction. Lilith had already known he was a well-favoured man. Now she had ample time to beat back her startled appreciation of the agreeable picture he made *en deshabille* before he shouted, 'Patterson,' in the general direction of the hall.

The butler reappeared in the open doorway. 'Sir?'

27

'I was under the impression I had informed you I was not at home.'

'You did indeed, sir,' the butler said, and withdrew to the hall, where Hester had been found a high-backed chair by one of his minions.

'You must not blame him,' said Lilith with a smile. 'I told him I knew very well you *were* at home, having just received a note from you. My name is Lilith Fitzgilbert. I wish to join your excavation proceedings in Newmarket. I do realise novice pupils are almost certainly a blight upon any serious landscape, so I propose paying for my instruction. If you are looking around for your coat, incidentally, it is on the back of that chair, but I beg you will not put it on just for me.'

Edward Makepeace immediately folded his arms and scowled as if to prove he'd had no such intention. A heavy ash-blond lock of hair fell across his forehead, destroying the forbidding look. 'Ditton Place is a bachelor establishment, madam. The work will be hard and there will be no room for niceties.'

A place where she could properly escape the social round. Lilith fought the desire to beam at him and instead gave an approving nod. 'That is excellent to hear. I have strong views on female education and deplore the practice of making allowances for ladies. You need not concern yourself over the proprieties. I shall be staying at a house in Newmarket for the next month, so will only be attending during the day. When do you travel?'

'As soon as possible. This is the family town house, and my sister-in-law is proposing to come up for a few days. Unfortunately, we do not know when, as none of us can decipher her appalling writing. We are thus making haste to vacate, which is why you find me amidst this confusion and why I gave orders that I was not at home.' His voice rose on the last phrase, clearly directed at the butler in the hall.

Lilith found his frustration surprisingly endearing and had to struggle not to smile. She had already espied a piece of cross-written, hot-pressed violet paper on one of the piles of books. How foolish of his sister-in-law. If there was one thing more calculated than any other to enrage the average male, it was the use of tinted paper. 'Ladies' handwriting is often difficult for gentlemen. Could your wife not relay the letter to you?'

'I am not married, madam.' The irritated look on his face said if she was a sample of English womanhood, he was never likely to be.

She smiled. 'Then may I see?' she asked. 'I may be able to help.'

'Miss Fitzgilbert, I regret that — '

'Ah, yes,' she said, studying the violet sheet, then turning it by ninety degrees and scanning the second set of lines. 'Mrs Henry Makepeace proposes joining you on the seventeenth, and trusts that the hangings in the blue bedchamber have been satisfactorily replaced, as she instructed in her letter of last month.'

'You can read that . . . that spider's web?' asked Mr Makepeace incredulously.

Lilith chuckled. 'Benedict considers it one of my most useful skills. My aunt travels extensively on the continent and has a habit of discovering promising artists, whom she despatches to us to launch into the London literati. Since she views any blank space on a page as an abomination, it became a matter of self-preservation some years ago to be able to interpret with utmost swiftness whatever missives she chose to share with us. Your brother and sister-in-law, incidentally, are bringing all their children, who are much looking forward to the treat of spending time with both their uncles.'

'Good God,' said her host faintly. He delved into the litter on his desk and produced a pocketbook. 'The seventeenth. That gives us four days. I am obliged to you, Miss Fitzgilbert.'

'Ned, have you seen my . . . oh, hello.'

Lilith turned. A slender young man, as fair and comely as Mr Makepeace, but finer-drawn and with a smile of singular sweetness, had hurried into the room. He extended an ink-stained hand for her to shake.

'Good evening,' she said. 'You are the other uncle, I take it?'

'My brother Richard,' said Edward Makepeace shortly. 'Ricky, this is Miss Fitzgilbert. Miss Fitzgilbert has deciphered Leonora's letter. They arrive here on Monday. Can you be ready to journey to Ditton Place in two days' time?'

'I can be ready tomorrow,' said Richard without hesitation. 'I will go and pack now.'

'I thought you were already packing?'

'I started, but then I had a marvellous idea for the second stanza so have been working on that instead.'

'You may read it to me in the carriage. Finish packing first.'

'I will. Goodbye, Miss Fitzgilbert.'

Lilith smiled. 'Goodbye. I daresay I will see you at Ditton Place.'

'Oh, famous. Will you be there too?'

The older Makepeace brother glared at her. 'No, she will not. I do not take female pupils.'

She burst out laughing. 'Come now, not even ones who can read cross-written letters and are excessively competent with regards to the sorting out of folios and books? A trial period of two weeks, shall we say? My brother can arrange payment immediately. Perhaps you had better write him a note to that effect, and I will take it with me to save your footman the trouble of delivering it.'

He glowered at her. 'Your grasp of facts is evidently shaky. How is your note-taking?'

'I have a distressingly logical mind for a female and have frequently been complimented on the legibility of my handwriting. Are you taking this treatise on Roman civilisations with you? I

33

should be most interested in reading it.'

He sighed, lifted the drawer, and extracted a sheet of paper and a pen from underneath it. Lilith was impressed. Mr Makepeace evidently knew exactly where everything was, despite the confusion. 'I will see you at Ditton Place no earlier than the seventeenth, Miss Fitzgilbert. Bring your maid for respectability, and stout clothing for both of you that does not object to mud and rain.' He wrote rapidly, shook sand over the sheet, folded it and handed it to her. 'Pray congratulate your brother on the loss of your company. Should you change your mind, you may assure yourself that I will not be in the least desolate.'

Lilith smiled. 'Until the seventeenth, Mr Makepeace. Come, Hester, we will need to re-examine our wardrobes.'

3

'Lord Fitzgilbert to see you, sir.'

Fitzgilbert. Ned looked up in alarm before his brain registered 'Lord' rather than 'Miss'. He breathed a cautious sigh of relief, hoping this was a visit from Miss Fitzgilbert's brother to say the lady had thought better of yesterday's impulse. He had already castigated himself half a dozen times since opening his eyes about unaccountably agreeing to her joining the proceedings in Newmarket. His excuse was that she had caught him at a disadvantage. Today, with last night's clutter crated and ready to go, he felt a good deal more in control. He stood and held out his hand as a tall, dark, perfectly-turned-out gentleman with his sister's grey-green eyes crossed the room towards him.

'Benedict Fitzgilbert,' said the other

man, shaking it. 'I thought I'd better come in person. I've read a couple of your articles in the *Gentleman's Magazine*, but I don't think we've run across each other particularly. Oxford man, I gather?'

This did not sound like a man making his sister's excuses; it sounded like an older brother interviewing an unknown antiquarian to ascertain for himself that he was genuine. Blast. 'I'm flattered you recognised my name, my lord. Will you take some refreshment? Yes, I attended Oxford. I have to keep quiet about that whenever I journey into Cambridgeshire.' He signalled to Patterson to bring the decanter of Madeira.

A faint frown crossed Fitzgilbert's face. 'Cambridgeshire? I understood your estate to be near Newmarket.'

Ned grinned. 'Which is of course in Suffolk. The county boundary runs through the town. Ditton Place is on the Cambridgeshire side, a matter of three miles away. It abuts the Duke of

Rutland's land, if you are familiar with the area. A family connection on my mother's side, many years ago.'

His visitor's expression cleared. 'Ah, I see. Oh, thank you. Very civil.' He sipped the wine the butler proffered and gave an approving nod. 'Well now, I have brought the sum required for my sister's first two weeks' tuition. You will find her an apt scholar. Could I trouble you for a receipt? My man of business is rarely moved to eloquence, but he made such an impassioned plea this morning that I feel obliged to take him back a billet of some kind. Are you sure Miss Fitzgilbert will not be in your way during the excavations?'

When Ned went over this scene in his head later, he could have sworn he had every intention of saying yes at this point and extricating himself from an awkward situation. 'I can always use an accurate note taker,' he found himself replying. 'I hope she is not anticipating treasures. I expect to find very little except different layers of soil, stones and other materials in the walls of the Ditch. It is the history and the construction and what it may tell us about the ancient builders that interests me.'

His visitor nodded. 'Lilith can certainly keep records. I should stress that she will be accompanied by her maid and one of my men. You are welcome to make use of the man, but his primary purpose will be to maintain my sister's safety.'

Ned couldn't imagine the poised, self-confident lady who had visited him yesterday needing anything bar her own personality to keep her safe, but he nodded. 'That is perfectly understandable. I would make the same stipulation, had I a sister.' He reached for a pen. 'I'm afraid the receipt will not be as full of elaborate words as the one my secretary would have written. I hope to be off within twenty-four hours, and Kerr gave me firmly to understand that the shortness of notice in which to assemble his belongings meant I should only disturb him in a dire emergency.'

Lord Fitzgilbert winced in sympathy. 'Sometimes you wonder who employs whom, don't you? You must be wishing me at the devil, so I'll take my leave. Your brother accompanies you?'

Why would he be asking about Ricky? 'My younger brother, yes. I am, in effect, his guardian. My older brother's imminent descent on this house, complete with his family, has much to do with our precipitous exodus.'

At this, Lord Fitzgilbert gave a laugh. 'Then I shall certainly not keep you. I may run across you in Newmarket. Good day.'

Ned was left with the impression of a disquieting intelligence, a warm smile, and — like his sister — a pleasant but implacable will. He finished his own glass of Madeira and looked at the roll of banknotes Fitzgilbert had left on the desk. Hell and damnation, he was going to *have* to set up an excavation now.

'Patterson,' he said, striding out to the hall, 'I'm going to the Society of Antiquaries.' One thing about Somerset House was that there were always hopeful scholars littering the rooms who might be tempted by the Cambridgeshire air and a little practical experience.

His butler didn't move. 'Yes, sir. In that coat, sir?'

Ned took a deep breath. 'Yes, in this coat. I like this coat. It is comfortable. It does not require the aid of two footmen to insert me into it. If I once take it off, Ferris will apologetically tell me he mislaid it whilst packing, yet when we return to London, it will be nowhere in sight.'

'Very good, sir.'

Ned collected his hat and gloves from a footman whose face was contorted with the struggle not to laugh. 'Console yourself, Patterson, with the reflection that after tomorrow Mr Richard and I will no longer be here to disgrace you. Your standing in the butlers' network will improve substantially. My elder brother and his wife have never yet set foot out of doors wearing anything but their finest.'

He chuckled as he ran down the steps. Poor Patterson. He hadn't even given the butler time to tell the footman to summon a hackney. Just as well. At this time of day, it was as easy to walk. He didn't really give a damn if anyone thought him eccentric.

★ ★ ★

Somerset House always had an air of purpose about it, with three learned societies based there as well as the stamp office and various naval departments. Today it was unusually busy.

'Didn't you hear?' said his friend Thornley with a laugh when Ned commented on the unwonted activity. 'The Royal Academy Stranger Day lecture yesterday was infiltrated by a female, so they are doubling all the porters and enjoying themselves immensely by saying they don't know what the world is coming to. I always knew they were a set of loose screws over on that side of the arch.'

'I can't see why they'd worry,' said Ned. 'Two of the founding members of the Royal Academy were women. How are they ever going to admit more if they don't teach them?'

'Oh, they don't mind teaching them in their own studios for a suitable fee, just not within these hallowed walls. Keep the dear creatures in their place.'

As Ned knew precisely where his friend's idea of a woman's place was, he declined to pursue the argument, merely saying, 'It seems absurd to me to make such a fuss.'

'I didn't know you had liberal tendencies, Makepeace.'

Ned shrugged. 'Ability is ability. Talking of which, have you got any young hopefuls who could spend a few days in Cambridgeshire scraping away at my Ditch? Henry and Leonora are coming to town with the family, so

42

Ricky and I are escaping to Newmarket tomorrow and I'm thinking of running a short training school ready for the summer.'

'Splendid idea. The sooner the men get used to the routine, the better. I've got a class this morning. I'll ask them. Usual arrangements? Board and lodging provided in return for labour?'

'Yes, but they find their own way there.'

'I can only let you have them for a week. I've got a guest lecture set up the following Tuesday.'

Perfect, thought Ned. Miss Fitzgilbert would be thoroughly bored by then. And, he remembered with a queasy start, he had to be back in London himself by the twenty-sixth for the dinner he was holding for potential investors in his Greek project. He'd have to leave a note to that effect for Leonora. He wondered if he could get away with staying for one night only. 'After a few days in my Ditch, they'll attend to him like little lambs,' he said.

'Leave it with me. Expect them next week. Oh, and don't go poaching them for Greece. They're coming with me to Egypt.'

Ned clapped him on the shoulder. 'You're all heart, Thornley.'

As he walked back, he ran over the list of things he had yet to do and found it pleasingly small. There was no reason why they shouldn't set out early tomorrow. It was always difficult leaving the busyness of Somerset House for the country, but now the decision had been made, he was looking forward to seeing Ditton Place again. It would get Ricky out of town for one thing, and for another there must be several crates of books and other artefacts that he'd had sent there and not yet unpacked. They would all need sorting out. *Several* crates. He realised with a twinge of guilt that he'd not set eyes on the estate since departing for Egypt in the spring.

* * *

A day later, Ned's sanguine mood had altered considerably. His temper had been dangerously short, in fact, ever since they had arrived at Ditton Place mid-afternoon to find unkempt lawns, a weed-infested drive, and the house itself in nothing like the state he had left it seven months ago.

He pushed his plate away before indigestion ceased to be merely threatening and became violent. 'Mrs Bell's cooking has not improved, I see,' he said.

His brother, who had been eating one-handed whilst making frowning jabs with his pencil at his latest epic poem, looked up vaguely. 'Hasn't it?' He glanced at his meal in a puzzled fashion, shrugged and ate the final forkful.

Ned's secretary sat back from his likewise empty plate. 'I noticed nothing amiss,' he said in his precise fashion. 'It was wholesome and filling. Do you require me this evening? I still have a considerable amount to unpack.'

With wafts of disapproval drifting

down from his rooms the whole time because I've moved us from London to the countryside. 'Take the evening to get yourself settled, Kerr. I have crates in plenty myself to sort out in the library. Tell me, Atkins, is there anything at all fit to drink in this house?' *And if not, where has it gone? For I know I bought a dozen of a very decent burgundy when I was last here, which should have matured nicely by now.*

The butler moved towards the decanter. 'The wine, sir . . . '

'Is not what I left here in the spring.'

Ned said it pleasantly, but there was an edge to his voice that must have been obvious to the meanest intelligence. It seemed Atkins's intelligence did not extend even that far. The butler — whom Ned hadn't particularly liked when Kerr had engaged him at the beginning of the year — assumed a sorrowful demeanour. 'All turned to vinegar, sir.'

'Dear me,' said Ned. 'It was thus

doubtless given to Mrs Bell to use in the kitchen, was it? For the preserving of vegetables, perhaps? I remember dining on a rather fine ragout in France which I was assured was made with a red wine vinegar. Perhaps the kitchen could oblige me with a dish of the same tomorrow?'

Atkins bowed. 'I shall convey your wishes to Mrs Bell.'

'Not to the housekeeper? Do we no longer have one? It would explain why the rooms were so ill-prepared.'

'Mrs Gunn is on an errand of mercy to her sister. A broken leg, I understand. Mrs Bell has kindly been deputising for her in addition to her normal duties.'

'Not very well, it seems.'

'With respect, sir, we had very little notice of your arrival.'

'You should not need any,' snapped Ned. 'I pay you to keep Ditton Place in order the year round and you have had precious little to do over the past few months. Kerr, you had better visit the

47

registry office in Newmarket first thing on Monday.'

The butler shot a veiled look at Ned's secretary.

'It is likely to be a cold winter, sir,' interposed Kerr in a detached tone. 'If you were minded to extend the servants a day or so to reflect on that fact, it may well be you would see an improvement in standards.'

Ned strode over to the fire and kicked it forcefully into life. He was being robbed by his butler, his house was staffed by incompetents, and any moment now he was going to give in.

It will be a cold winter.

Damn Kerr. He had meant it as a subtle threat to Atkins, but he couldn't have known the effect it would have on Ned himself.

He could feel everybody's eyes on his back. 'Very well,' he said. 'Twenty-four hours. I am now going to the library, and I do not wish to be disturbed. Ricky, come with me and make yourself useful.'

★ ★ ★

Ned watched his valet closely as the man hung up his evening coat. It was one of his favourites, being comfortable and warm. In Ned's experience, those two factors were all that were needed for his clothes to mysteriously vanish. 'Have you discovered the reason behind the state of the house?' he asked. 'I'm assuming Atkins is either lazy or a rogue, but is there something else?'

Ferris didn't turn a hair. 'Difficult to say, sir. The staff — such as they are — fall silent whenever I'm in the room.'

'No doubt overawed by your superior town airs. Try asking at the inn in the village. The landlord's a decent sort, as I recall.'

A very faint smile flitted across the valet's face. 'As it happens, observing how flustered Mrs Bell appeared to be at our arrival, I suggested to Mr Chilcott that he and the other grooms repair to the Three Blackbirds for their evening meal to ease the strain on the kitchen.'

Ned nodded. 'Very good, Ferris. Very good indeed. I'll go to the stables first thing to check on the horses. I also need to refresh my memory on the earthworks.'

'I have already laid out your riding clothes.'

'And procured a warming pan for the bed, I see. Well done. Did we know Mrs Gunn had a sister?'

'I have never heard her speak of one, sir.'

'Nor me, which is strange as she has been here these twenty years.' Ned stretched. 'I wish Locke hadn't asked to be pensioned off last Christmas. After what I've seen today, I don't trust Atkins an inch. I won't need you any more tonight, Ferris. You might take a look at Mr Richard before you turn in. I've tried to wear him out this evening, but there's no saying he won't get an idea about that blasted poem into his head and then sit up all night working on it.'

'You may depend on me, sir.'

'Just as well,' remarked Ned to the door panel once it was safely closed. 'I don't think I've made too many other friends in this house since we arrived.'

4

Lilith looked out of her first-floor bedchamber window at the flat Cambridgeshire landscape. The journey had not been particularly fatiguing, and below her, Benedict and Nicholas Dacre were already walking across the Furze House yard towards the stables, talking hard. She exhaled softly. She had three weeks, maybe four, with no one to please and no one to organise but herself. The unaccustomed freedom was dizzying. She could hardly believe it. 'I don't think I have ever seen so much sky as there is in this part of the world,' she remarked aloud to cover her thoughts. 'Not on land. At sea it is different, one expects it.'

Catherine Redding joined her at the window. Catherine was her friend Verity's older sister, but they had been estranged for several years so Lilith didn't really know her. 'Extraordinary, isn't it?' she said. 'I forgot this sky when I was in London. Coming back was like taking a deep breath. I could feel myself expand. Will this room suit you? This one and your brother's next door must have been used by the previous tenants, for they are far grander than the rest. The saloon is also on this floor, at the front of the house. My sitting room is downstairs. You may spread your belongs around up here entirely as you please. We have become adept at moving furniture about, so if there is anything missing, do please say.'

Lilith glanced around. Hester had already unpacked, giving the room a touch of home. 'It is charming. From what Verity reported, I was expecting to refurbish the whole house.'

'Oh, there is a lot of that to do, especially the other wing. Let me show you the saloon first, then we can go and look at it. We are calling it the Gentleman's Wing for the moment, largely to satisfy the townsfolk who view a ladies' lodging house with deep suspicion.' She paused. 'Though that may be because they have met my friend Molly. By the by, if your maid and footman don't like the rooms I have put them in, there are any number of others they may choose. They need not be shy about changing.'

'Have no fear. Hester used to be my mother's maid and persists in treating me as a precocious twelve-year-old. I have never yet known her reticent, whether invited to speak her mind or not.' Lilith followed her hostess to the handsome saloon at the front of the house where her books and drawing board were waiting to be distributed about the room. She hesitated. 'Verity has told me of your history, Catherine. I know we are not to speak of your previous marriage nor mention your real name outside the house, for fear of your whereabouts travelling to Flint's ears, but is this truly what you want? To be — in effect — a housekeeper?'

In repose, Catherine was lovely.

When she smiled, beauty shone out of her. 'It really is. My being born a gentleman's daughter is insignificant. I long ago lost any claim to that life. Provided I am careful in my dealings with the neighbourhood, I am *safe* here and my daughter is safe. That is truly all that matters. As for this house, I have my room next to Ann upstairs, my sitting room downstairs, and my kitchen. The other rooms are filling up with Verity's waifs and strays, and she has also supplied me with two housemaids and an assistant cook from the Kennet End dower house. Given my prospects just a month ago, I am more than content. You will see for yourself it's not like being a housekeeper. At Furze House we all help each other.'

'The place runs on progressive lines, then?' said Lilith. 'My mother wrote a treatise on the subject once, but she could never persuade Papa to try it out in Bedford Square. Now I fear, with poor Benedict forced to remember he is a baron all the time, we will never be able to implement such a system. Even if we wanted to, the servants are far too much taken up with their own hierarchy and consequence.' She took a quick breath. 'There is something else I must say, this time as a friend. Forgive me, but I could not help noticing the warmth with which Mr Dacre addressed you. You do know he . . . ?'

'I do know, yes.' Catherine met her gaze, candid but unapologetic. 'There are many reasons why Nicholas and I cannot be always together, and that is the least of them. While he is here, I am his and he is mine. It is sufficient. Do you care to see over the house now?'

'I should like to, yes.' A movement from the window caught her eye. Below them, a cart was trundling between the gateposts, with a rosy, compact woman sitting on the perch next to the carter. 'You have a delivery, it seems.'

Catherine looked out. 'It is Molly,' she said, puzzled. 'Wait, there is someone on the bed of the cart. Oh my goodness, the poor woman!' Without further ado, she dashed for the door.

A domestic disturbance. At home, Lilith would have picked up a book and retired to a chair to read while her housekeeper set all to rights below. But ... *It's not like being a housekeeper. We all help each other here.* Wasn't that what Catherine had said?

Feeling oddly displaced, Lilith went out to the upper landing. Shouts for assistance could be heard downstairs. She descended to the ground floor and then, as the commotion was coming from the back premises, continued through the swinging baize door to a narrow passage. The side door to the yard stood open. As she reached it, a small girl pelted indoors, followed by the matron in charge of the laundry at the rear of the house, talking volubly as she got to the kitchen.

'The poor lady. You did quite right, Moll,' said the woman, who Lilith remembered was Ma Turner. 'Good thing we've not fitted out that back room for a servants' sitting room yet, eh? Let's get the poor soul in there. Run and get the old sheets, Peg. Now then, young Hannah, I'll want some warm water, not hot enough to scald. Can you do that? Good girl. We'll need a drop of gin too, I'm thinking.'

'No . . . '

As Lilith edged hesitantly around the kitchen door, she saw a middle-aged woman with pain lines etched into her face and the distended body shape that betokens the imminent arrival of a child. She was being helped to a chair, her eyes wild with fear.

'No spirits,' she gasped. 'That's how . . . that's how . . . '

Catherine's friend Molly Turner — she from the perch of the cart — exchanged a glance with her mother. 'Laudanum, then? She'll need something, poor soul. First kiddies ain't easy. You got a bottle, Kitty?'

Catherine shook her head. 'We dosed Nicholas with the last of it when we fixed his arm.'

'I . . . ' Lilith cleared her throat. 'I

can go to the apothecary to buy whatever is necessary, if someone will show me the way.'

Catherine smiled at her in quick relief. 'Would you? That would be kind. Molly's children will show you. It's not far and it will be quicker than sending one of them for Nicholas. As soon as gentlemen start talking about horses they lose track of days, let alone hours. Ask the apothecary for a mild tincture only. Tell him it is for a labouring woman.'

Luckily, the two small girls did indeed know where to go. Peg and Nell, she discovered, and they liked it fine in Newmarket, even though they hadn't been able to sleep at first, it was so quiet here after London. They chattered all the way down the High Street, then fell silent inside the shop, looking at the great glass jars lining the shelves and the sacks piled up underneath.

'No touching,' Lilith warned them, hoping that the apothecary would hurry and fulfil her request while the girls were still awed. She was not in the least used to children, and certainly not inquisitive ones.

The shopman did give the girls a sharp look, but listened civilly. 'A tincture of laudanum? Nothing easier. Furze House, you say? I'd heard that was a place for single females.'

'Yes indeed,' replied Lilith, nipping his very slight hint of disparagement in the bud. 'So many ladies have nowhere they can live without being dependent on their relations. It is a great boon to have a respectable house in the district where they may live quietly, but genteelly.'

Her unruffled calm had its effect. 'A blessing, miss,' he agreed. To the girls' fascination, he fetched out a jar labelled *Opium Tablets*, shook one into a mortar and ground it for a minute or so with the pestle, then weighed a pinch on a tiny pair of scales and whisked the powder in a jug before pouring the resultant tincture into a labelled bottle. 'Sixpence, please. If you need more, just send these little shavers up for you. I'll know them now.'

Lilith returned to a crescendo of screams from the back room. She swallowed. Should she go in, or simply leave the laudanum on the table and take herself off?

Peg and Nell had no such scruples. Lilith perforce followed them through the door. Catherine ran across. 'Thank you. I'll put a few drops into some lemonade for her. Molly says the carter found her doubled over by the side of the road. She was babbling about getting to *The Ladies' House*, which we think must be here, but of course he didn't know of it. He lifted her on to his cart and stopped at the Horseshoes to ask where a nurse might be found. Molly was in there looking for work, so told him to carry on driving straight here. Ma Turner thinks the poor woman has been in labour many hours already. The strength of her, to keep going! As soon as the babe's born, I'll get some broth down her. She's not young either, is she? Oh!'

They both turned at a sudden baby's cry. The woman herself was now panting and silent. Catherine's hand gripped Lilith's. 'It's just like when Ann was born,' she whispered and hunted for a handkerchief to dab her eyes.

'Is . . . is the babe all right . . . ?' The woman's voice was weak, painfully hopeful.

Lilith found her own throat closing over with emotion.

'A bonny girl with a fine pair of lungs on her,' said Ma Turner. 'One moment . . . there, take her now and give one last push that you'll never notice. Put her to suckle, Moll.'

Lilith couldn't move, fixing in her head the transfigured joy on the woman's lined, tear-stained face as she looked at her new daughter, lying against her breast. She needed to sketch this now, before the wonder permeating the whole room faded. Her fingers were burning to get to her pencil.

Catherine left the room with her.

'What will you be thinking? Furze House is not normally this lively, I assure you. I'll heat her some broth and a drink, then I'll bring you up some tea. Ann, come with me, and in a while you can help me make up a room upstairs for when she feels stronger. Let the poor woman rest for now.'

* * *

'Well, my dear, are you content? Can you be happy here?' asked Benedict as they parted that night after a superb meal. It had been cooked by Catherine, who then left her pots and pans to eat with them. Nicholas Dacre made up the fourth at the table.

'I shall be well fed, and there is certainly enough to do,' she answered. 'I believe this can be a comfortable house, if that's what you mean.'

'It is not what I mean, and you know it.'

She did, but she could hardly say she was looking forward to this respite from her normal life without making her brother feel guilty for monopolising so much of her time in London. In truth, she had had a lovely afternoon, working on the drawing of Mrs Smith and her new daughter. No inner voice reminding her that she should be running through guest lists for Ben's next dinner, or planning menus for a soirée, or curbing her stepmother's more flamboyant schemes for redesigning the principal rooms in Bedford Square. Perfect.

'Peace, Benedict. I will be well enough. Furze House is unconventional, but it is also stimulating, and I would be a feeble creature if my mind was not flexible enough to cope. Hester is more likely to suffer from the unorthodox arrangements than I am. Will you walk around the house with me tomorrow to see what needs setting in train?'

'Certainly. I had a brief tour with Nick this afternoon. He tells me the local furniture broker already regards him as a favourite customer. If the excavation at Ditton Place turns out to be not as you expect, do not feel obliged to stay. There will be enough and more to occupy your hours here.'

'I may remain long enough to investigate Mr Makepeace's library. Do you realise there is not a single book in Furze House except those I brought with me?'

Her brother looked amused. 'Well, and why should there be, when up until now it has always been let out to tenants? I have every confidence that by the time I return to collect you, you will have organised the local carpenter to build bookcases in one of the empty rooms and plundered all the bookshops in a twenty-mile radius to fill them.'

Now that was not a bad plan at all, mused Lilith, sitting down at her dressing table and submitting to Hester's ministrations with the hairbrush. Licence to go searching out booksellers. She basked again in the joy of being her own mistress. Really, if she'd known the consequences of scandal were going to be this pleasant, she would have borrowed Benedict's clothes and infiltrated the Royal Academy Schools long ago.

5

Ned woke to the cheerful crackle of a fire in the grate and a rattle of rings around the bed as his curtains were drawn back.

'Good morning, Ferris. What time is it?'

'Seven-thirty, sir, and a satisfactory amount of work taking place in the kitchen, though not as full a complement of staff as there used to be. If you wish to investigate your earthworks early, I am confident there will be an adequate breakfast available on your return. The church service this week is the evening one.'

Ned stretched lazily and grinned. Ferris was a wonder. 'Did you discover that from Atkins or Chilcott?'

'Neither, sir. The young footman downstairs is a native of the village.'

'Then I hope he and the other

servants will attend and enhance the standing of Ditton Place. I must pay a courtesy visit to Rutland, so I may remain there. Is my brother with the world yet? I should take him to Cheveley with me.'

'I was going to wake him after I had seen to you, sir.'

Half an hour later, Ned was ruefully surveying the collapsed earthfall that in the spring had been a perfectly good site of investigation. The steady rain of the summer had not only taken its toll of the crops, it had also weakened the bracing he had put in.

'Back to last year's site,' he announced over breakfast. 'I had a feeling we were digging too close to the start of the dyke in the spring. Ricky, can you be ready to start tomorrow morning? I've asked Chilcott to help us and told him to detail a couple of the gardeners to ready the site. That's assuming we still have any gardeners, which seems doubtful given the state of the lawns.'

He glanced at the butler, standing correctly by the chafing dishes and giving no sign of having heard him. 'Atkins, there will be a group of scholars arriving in the next day or so. When is Mrs Gunn expected to return?'

His tone was cordial, but a wary look came into Atkins's eyes. 'She did not say, sir.'

Nor, according to Chilcott, had any of the stable hands driven her into Newmarket to catch the stage. Indeed, they could not remember when they had last seen her. More and more he wanted Atkins out of his employ. 'That seems unlike her. When did she leave?'

'I . . . last week, I believe.'

Ned inspected a dish of eggs, none of which he was in the least tempted to introduce to his stomach. 'You believe?'

'I cannot remember the exact day.'

Ned looked at the man for a long moment. 'Remind me again why I employ you?'

Atkins darted a glance around the

room. 'If I am not giving satisfaction, I should prefer a private interview, sir.' The request was reasonable, but there was an odd note in his voice.

Kerr rose to his feet. 'Will I draft an advertisement for a new housekeeper?' he asked.

Ned bit back his annoyance. There was often a Calvinistic quality to Donald Kerr's efficiency. No doubt he wanted to clear business out of the way before he left for whichever church suited his hell-fire-and-eternal-damnation observances, but did he have to be quite so blind to atmosphere? The interruption had given Atkins time to recover his composure. There would be little point having an interview with him now. 'It seems premature when Mrs Gunn has previously given satisfaction. Atkins, instruct the housemaids to prepare half a dozen rooms. And if you could convey a request to Mrs Bell for drinkable coffee, I would appreciate it.'

Meanwhile he addressed himself to the loaf of bread, which had the merit of having arrived via the baker's boy, and a plate of bacon which even Mrs Bell had failed to render inedible. If his Grace extended an invitation to him and Ricky to stay for supper at Cheveley, he would accept it in the manner of a drowning man sighting a friendly fishing boat.

★   ★   ★

The unconventionality of Furze House did not extend to a lack of church observance, though the watchfulness with which Nicholas Dacre observed everyone in the vicinity was a reminder that Catherine was still in danger from Flint. Afterwards, Lilith was detailed to keep Mrs Smith company while a bedchamber was prepared, and to stop her from carrying anything more than her sewing upstairs.

'Such a trouble I am being,' said the woman. She was quiet and well-spoken. Her fingers were nimble as she set a narrow strip of old lace ribbon into a nightgown for her child.

'Not at all,' replied Lilith. 'The men are enjoying themselves immensely moving your furniture. I have been admiring your handiwork. Your stitching is beautiful.'

She got a quick smile. 'I have been doing little else this last month. The friends I was staying with are elderly and have scant money for new furnishings. A table runner and a set of seat covers was the least I could do in return for their kindness in taking me in. I lost my previous position when . . . ' She made a comprehensive gesture involving the nightgown and her child.

'Yes, quite. Mrs Redding tells me you have offered your needlework skills here. We are grateful, for there is a lot to be done.'

'I will be glad to. I was so pleased when word reached us of Furze House. I only wish I had heard of it sooner. My friends are dear creatures, but they live very quietly. A child in the house would have been a considerable upheaval for them. Here I am on equal terms. It has been such a comfort to meet the others and realise I am not the only female foolish enough be taken in by pretty words and a hidden motive.'

The exchange gave Lilith to think. She had at first been sceptical of her friend Verity's idea for a ladies' boarding house, but it had many merits. Her own mother had advocated something in the same style years ago, though her plan had been more for a blue-stocking establishment where ladies of intelligence could work without interruption. It had not occurred to Lilith that the sisterhood itself was as appealing as the roof over the inhabitants' heads.

The afternoon brought visitors, Catherine's brother and his wife. 'They will have come to meet you,' said Catherine with a sigh. 'Heaven knows how Selena has heard of your arrival, but where her coterie is concerned, no title passes unnoticed. It is the only time Verity or I are of any use.'

'It's Benedict who has the title, not me,' objected Lilith.

'You are the sister of a lord. She'll take crumbs just as well as a loaf.' Then, as Woods showed the visitors in, 'My dear Selena, you should not have come out in your condition. Do take this chair, it is by far the most comfortable. Lilith, may I present my sister-in-law Mrs Bowman. Selena, my friend Miss Fitzgilbert.'

Mrs Bowman replied artlessly that just fancy that, her friend Mrs Ives had mentioned seeing a prodigiously elegant lady and gentleman at St Mary's this morning, but she had had no idea they might be staying with her dear John's sister!

'We go to the service at Kennet End, of course,' she added. 'Such a comfort, having a family pew there.'

'Indeed,' agreed Lilith, straight-faced. 'Though I do find it makes it more difficult to notice any newcomers.'

'Oh no, for you see them afterwards,' said Mrs Bowman eagerly. 'We had a very smart sort of gentleman this morning. A Mr Fraser. He was most interested to hear of all the notable families in the district, and said at once ours must be a large household for we looked the most distinguished. It made it a little awkward telling him there were only the two of us. I was sorry Mama had a cold and felt herself unequal to attend church. A very polite gentleman, for all I had difficulty making out some of what he said. Reverend Milsom asked him if he was making a stay locally, but he said he was just passing through on his way north.'

'Probably lost,' muttered John Bowman. 'Ah, Dacre, just the man. Have you thought any more about taking one of my dogs?'

★ ★ ★

'The building is handsome,' observed Lilith on Monday morning as the Furze House carriage, which had until lately been a London hackney cab, clopped in a sedate fashion up the Ditton Place drive. Edward Makepeace's Queen Anne manor sat in a landscaped lawn, welcoming without being ostentatious, red-brick and pleasingly symmetrical in the morning sun.

Hester sniffed. 'I daresay the gardeners are all at work on these ruins, are they?'

Lilith chuckled. 'The Devil's Ditch is not a ruin, it is an earthwork ridge. But yes, this avenue is in desperate need of tidying and the pond should not be so choked with leaves, even though it is shockingly windy. It is possible Mr Makepeace does not spend much time here.'

'All the more reason it should be in order,' countered Hester. 'What else have the gardeners got to do?'

At the front door, Lilith's footman jumped smartly down from his seat by the driver and handed her out.

'Thank you, Woods. Now then, Mr Grimes, will you return for me at three o'clock?'

The driver touched his hat cheerfully. 'That I will, miss. It'll still be light enough for us to get back at that time without turning a hoof on a stone. Come on, old girl. Let's get home and see what else they've got for us to do. This is the life, eh?'

Woods, meanwhile, had ascended the three steps to the door and was beating a smart tattoo with the knocker.

'It's going to be a long walk back,' remarked Hester after a minute or two when the summons elicited no response. There was a certain *I knew it* quality to her tone that Lilith ignored.

Woods rapped again. 'I'll step around the back, shall I, Miss Fitzgilbert?'

'I think you had better, yes. No, wait, someone has heard you.'

The door opened and a very young footman stared worriedly at them. 'Yes?' he said.

Lilith stepped out of the wind into a pleasant, if sadly dusty, hall. 'Good morning. I have come to study with Mr Makepeace. Could you let him know

Miss Fitzgilbert has arrived?'

The footman gulped. His gaze hunted around the hall and settled rather desperately on the one person who was clearly a higher authority.

'Show the ladies into a room with a fire, lad,' said Woods, responding to the mute appeal. 'Then let your master know.'

'The library's got a good fire,' essayed the footman.

'That'll be where Miss Fitzgilbert can wait, then,' said Woods. 'Your first post, is it?'

The lad nodded. 'Mr Atkins was showing me what to do. But he's loped off.'

This was moderately alarming intelligence. Lilith exchanged a look with Woods. 'The library sounds ideal,' she said. 'I shall be quite happy waiting there.' Next to her, Hester gave a portentous sigh. Lilith threw her a quelling glance. 'Everyone has to learn,' she murmured.

'It's through here, miss.'

Lilith didn't register the comfortable chairs or even notice the fire. She had eyes for nothing except the bays of books. So many books. 'Wonderful,' she breathed. 'Woods, perhaps you could accompany . . . '

'Peter, miss. Peter Swann.'

'Perhaps you could accompany Peter in search of Mr Makepeace. It will enable you to discover the layout of Ditton Place.' *And why it is so disorganised.*

Woods gave an efficient nod.

'Mr Atkins is the butler, one assumes,' said Lilith. 'I wonder where he has *loped off* to?'

'Same place as the housekeeper and all the maids,' remarked Hester, looking disparagingly at the film of dust covering everything. 'I'm thinking you shouldn't have sent Fred Grimes back so fast. It's a good fire, though, I'll give him that.'

'Never mind the dust, consider the books,' said Lilith with satisfaction. She crossed to the nearest bookcase and perused the shelves. 'Mr Makepeace may take as long as he likes.'

It was just as well Lilith was content, for it was a good twenty minutes before Woods reappeared with a flustered maid in tow, bearing a tea tray and some slices of bread and butter.

'Mr Makepeace is at the site,' he said. 'Peter's gone to find him. Thank you, Lucy. Off you go back now.'

The maid threw him a look of mingled awe and hero-worship and scurried away.

'You have made quite an impression, Woods,' said Lilith, watching this byplay with amusement. 'Have you discovered why the house is in disarray?'

'The butler appears to have departed overnight. His room is empty and his belongings gone. I gather Mr Makepeace has been expressing himself forcefully regarding the condition of the house, which may be the reason. Additionally, the cook has taken the news so poorly that I feel sorry for anyone dining here today.'

Lilith blinked. 'The butler has absconded? Then why is Mr Make-peace at work on his site? It seems eccentric to say the least.'

'The general consensus is that the master doesn't know he's gone. If he did, he'd be striding around raising hell.'

'Language,' muttered Hester, putting down the mending she had provided herself with and picking up the teapot.

'How invigorating,' said Lilith. 'I wonder why it ever occurred to me that life in the country was dull. This is almost as exciting as the unexpected birth at Furze House.' She accepted a cup of tea and went back to reading her antiquarian journal.

★   ★   ★

Ned strode into his library holding on to his temper by a hair's breadth. 'What's this about Atkins? Where is Mr Kerr?' he demanded of the footman by the door. He paused, focusing properly. 'You're not one of my footmen.' *For a start, the man looked as if he actually knew what he was doing.*

'No, sir. I accompanied Miss Fitzgilbert. I will endeavour to locate Mr Kerr for you.' He bowed a lot more smoothly than any of Ned's legitimate staff and effaced himself.

Miss Fitzgilbert? The scene in London came back to him, along with an arrow-shaft of impending doom. He swivelled to the fireplace. A no-nonsense maid sat in an upright chair, a pair of amber evening gloves in her lap and a threaded needle in her hand, regarding him with disfavour. Miss Fitzgilbert herself was curled up in his own favourite chair, reading. The scene, though undoubtedly peaceful, filled him with foreboding.

'What the devil are you doing here?'

The maid's lips pursed in disapproval. Miss Fitzgilbert looked up from the comfortable depths of the chair. 'It is the seventeenth, is it not? Therefore I am here. This article is fascinating. I had no idea so many of our good roads were built by the Romans, though on reflection, I suppose they must have been built by someone. We seem to have lost the way of it in country areas. Were the Romans here before your Ditch or after it?'

He answered automatically. 'Before, I think, though the Anglo-Saxons certainly added to the height of the dyke later. My belief is the original earthworks were in the light of a barrier to make it easier to regulate the traffic and trade along the London road. Others think the Saxon tribes built the whole. The Ditch runs crosswise, cutting off the open fens from the woods. There were lawless elements on both sides, even with the Roman legions stationed along it, so it was an effective barrier against raids.' He caught himself. What was he *doing*? This was no time for a lecture.

Miss Fitzgilbert nodded intelligently, closed the journal and uncurled her legs, giving a brief, unsettling glimpse of ankle. 'I shall be most interested to see it. Shall we go now?'

There was nothing Ned would have liked better than to turn straight around and return to the site. 'It would give me great pleasure,' he said. 'Unfortunately, I have to deal with a defaulting butler. I must beg your pardon for a wasted journey, but I had best ask for your carriage to be called. Another day is unlikely to affect progress on the site.'

'I am afraid that won't be possible,' she said with a smile. 'Mr Grimes does not return for us until three o'clock.'

Ned held on to his patience. 'Then I shall order my carriage for you. I cannot devote . . . '

He was interrupted by Miss Fitzgilbert's footman, who had returned as noiselessly as any town servant. 'Mr Kerr is not in the house, sir. I am told he requested the carriage to go into Newmarket earlier this morning.'

'Did he indeed? And I suppose you can tell me why, can you?' Too late, he remembered the man was not one of his own servants.

'Your valet understands your secretary had visiting the bank in mind.'

Blast. Ned remembered Kerr had made some mention of that yesterday, along with an implied criticism that they had left town too precipitously for him to have drawn sufficient funds out in advance. 'I daresay it is too much to hope that he visits the registry office at the same time and requests a new butler,' he said sourly. 'I really cannot expect to run an antiquarian survey without either a butler or a housekeeper to see to the house.'

'No indeed,' agreed Miss Fitzgilbert warmly. She exchanged a look with her maid. 'I told you there would be a logical explanation, Hester. If there is no housekeeper, it would explain the dust. I imagine no one has told the maids how to go on. They are very young, after all.'

Were they? Ned experienced a moment of guilt, trying to bring any of them to mind. Annoyance jabbed him that she had noticed immediately what he had not.

Miss Fitzgilbert stood. 'Woods, may I have my outdoor wear? Your brother and some of the men are at the site, I assume, Mr Makepeace?'

Now what was she about? 'That is correct,' he said cautiously, if by 'some of the men', she meant Chilcott. 'Ricky is not an antiquarian, but he makes a good assistant.'

'I will be interested to renew my acquaintance with him. Meanwhile Woods can continue Peter's instruction in the duties of a footman whilst he waits for your secretary to return with the carriage, and Hester can advise the maids on how to thoroughly clean a room. She'll enjoy that far more than a muddy walk and it will produce visible results which is always pleasing.'

'This is quite impossible, Miss Fitzgilbert. I appreciate that having paid for a course of tuition you are entitled to receive it, but . . . '

86

She gave him a tolerant smile. 'You must see that with no vehicles between us, I cannot return to Newmarket. You will feel more settled getting on with some work in the knowledge that a comfortable room awaits your return. And before you argue that you should be discovering what has become of your butler, let me point out that Woods is far better placed than you to find out when Mr Atkins was last seen and what sort of mood he was in. In my experience, employers are the very last people to be informed when something untoward has happened below stairs.'

Ned looked at her in exasperation. Everything she said had the merit of common sense. This was infuriating as he couldn't think of a counter-argument even though he *knew* she was wrong. Very well, he would hurry her to the Ditch, show her the workings, and then load her down with reading matter and be rid of her for the day.

'Are you always so managing, Miss Fitzgilbert?' he asked as they retraced his steps to the site.

She smiled, ignoring his irascible tone. 'Won't you call me Lilith? It will be easier if we are to work together.'

Lilith. Using her given name was unconventional, but if she was serious in her intention to be here every day — and he began to worry she might be — he could not be *Miss Fitzgilbert*-ing her all that time. Yes, it was best to move to informality now, then she would not read anything into it when he forgot and addressed her by name. 'Very well. I am Edward. My friends call me Ned.' *Amongst other things.*

'Thank you. I apologise if I seemed peremptory. It often takes someone at a distance from the problem to see events straight. It did not seem to me any good could come of your agitating your household before all the facts are known. Your secretary may already have the problem in hand, and is simply sparing you the knowledge of it until he can provide you with the solution.'

He frowned. 'It would be like Kerr,

but if something is wrong in my house I should be the one to deal with it. The privilege of being the master should not mean I shirk all responsibility, whatever my natural inclination might be.'

'I assure you, Woods will discover what your responsibility is far quicker than you might. You may then make as many decisions on how to rectify it as you please.'

'Thank you. That is very comforting. I own, when your brother said I might make use of your footman, this was not quite what I foresaw.'

'Why no, how could you? But Woods is kind and capable. That is why I brought him with me. He should be in a higher position than senior footman, only our butler at home is also very capable and is likely to continue in his post many years yet. My brother has an interest in Furze House, and it was in my mind that Woods might like the place well enough to take up a similar post there. However, the house is being run on quite different lines. It is more of a cooperative endeavour amongst residents.'

Despite his resolve to simply show her the workings and be done, Ned's interest was caught. 'A progressive establishment?'

'Yes, it is an admirable aim, but I cannot see how it would work for someone like me. In general I am so busy running Benedict's public life that my own time is preciously guarded. I came to the mortifying conclusion on the very day of my arrival in Newmarket that — much as I deplore certain aspects of society and do most earnestly believe in greater equality — I am too selfish to wholeheartedly back a revolution.'

Without at all intending to, Ned found himself chuckling. He helped her across the planks he had laid down on a muddy part of the path and said, 'What happened to warrant such a reflection?'

She turned a rueful countenance to him. 'The most bizarre occurrence. An unknown lady arrived at the house, perilously close to being confined, having been discovered in great distress by a carter at the side of the road. No one made the least demur about taking her in, but all set about making the poor woman comfortable and then helped to deliver the child.'

Ned was startled. 'Even though she was a stranger?'

'Yes. It made no difference to their care.'

He tried to imagine a similar thing happening at the town house. And failed. 'I can see why you would be astonished, but you would surely not have turned the woman away had it been left to you?'

'Naturally not, but what made the biggest impression was that *everyone* helped without question. Such a thing was out of my experience, so immediate and so close. I felt . . . I felt superfluous.'

He gave a short laugh. 'As I do now with Atkins missing, the house in confusion and nothing I can do to any purpose.'

'Why no, for as soon as the facts in your butler's case are ascertained it will be your part to act. All *I* could do was go to the apothecary for laudanum.'

'I am sure that was appreciated.'

She looked at him frankly. 'The task could have been done by anyone. The small girls from the laundry who showed me the way could have easily gone by themselves. I felt envy, I think, that the household knew what to do and worked as a group. To my shame I also thought if that sort of thing happened every day, I should never get any work of my own done at all.'

Ned laughed aloud. 'You are refreshingly honest and clear-sighted. Whether you intended it or not, I now feel much better about myself. The Devil's Ditch is on the other side of these trees. The path is muddy and rutted, so if you care to take my arm, I will guide you through the wood here instead.'

6

For a man of learning, Edward Makepeace had a very firm arm — clearly the manual labour of excavation was extraordinarily beneficial when it came to a man's physique. It was certainly a masterful experience having his aid across the woodland floor. Lilith puzzled over how she might convey that strength and agility in a drawing. Perhaps the muscles themselves could give her a clue? In her mind's eye she replaced Sir Thomas Lawrence's model with Edward — and then flushed to the roots of her hair at the thought of him reclining naked on a dais.

'Careful,' said Edward, keeping her upright with that same firm arm as she momentarily forgot how her feet worked and tripped headlong over a fallen branch. 'I should have reminded you to watch out under the trees. I am afraid Atkins must have alienated the outdoor staff as well as the indoor servants. The paths should all be much clearer than they are.'

'It was my fault entirely,' said Lilith, shutting the door on her imaginary life-drawing class with considerable haste. At least the stumble had provided a reason for her sudden rapid breathing.

And then they came out of the small wood and Lilith stopped breathing altogether. The long, towering ridge of the Devil's Ditch stretched away in the distance as far as she could see and must have been at least four times a man's height. She stood there in amazement, still clasping Edward's arm, and craned her neck backwards to look higher. And higher still.

'I'm sorry, I should have warned you,' he said, not sounding sorry at all but, on the contrary, rather pleased at the effect the massive earthwork had on her.

'It is extraordinary. How tall is it? However did they make it?'

'The dyke is some twenty-five foot from the ground to the top at this point. The ditch itself runs along the far side. That is about fifteen foot deep. It is logical to assume they dug bucket-loads of soil from the ditch and deposited them on the top, over and over again, for the whole length of the dyke. The strata in the section we have excavated seems to indicate as much.'

Lilith pictured the scene, peopling it with Roman soldiers and native villagers, all working together. 'Thus creating a barrier and a ditch in one. Every bucketful increases both height and depth. How clever.'

'It would have made an effective defence, as long as it was manned. The ridge is broad enough to walk along. Soldiers or warriors would have had patrols guarding it. A few small coins that we judge to have been Roman have been found.'

'How does one attain the top?' asked

Lilith, looking up at it again.

He raised an eyebrow. 'One walks along to where I have previously cut steps into the side of the bank. I left my brother and my groom there, hopefully labelling the soil types and sifting it for tools or artefacts.'

But when they reached the rough-hewn steps, there was no sign of Richard Makepeace, though the site working was evident.

Edward frowned. 'Confound the boy. Where is he? I hope Chilcott is with him.'

Above the noise of the wind, Lilith thought she could hear what at one of her stepmother's soirées would be stirring poetry. 'On the ridge?' she suggested. 'I believe somebody is reciting up there.'

Edward looked resigned. 'That will be Ricky. Imagining himself by turns a general, an aide-de-camp and a humble soldier. And not thinking at all of the wind that might knock him into the ditch at any moment.'

chalk and clay as we go higher. On the ditch side, the bands are mirrored above and below the good soil, lending substance to my theory about the construction.'

'Agreeable, to find yourself proved right.'

'Strong conjecture, rather than proof. We will get on faster once the scholars arrive. I had started another excavation near the beginning of the dyke which shows promising evidence of a guard post or some such, but the rain over the summer has caused it to collapse.'

Lilith watched as he took off his low-crowned beaver to rub his temple and frown at the earth bank. Unlike the majority of the gentlemen in Benedict's set, Edward appeared to dress for comfort rather than fashion, not bothered that his coat was two seasons old or that his hair was now being tousled by the wind in a most distracting manner. It was only ash blond on the top, Lilith realised. The lower layers were shot through with corn gold and dark honey. It was a fascinating combination. Also decidedly unfair.

'It has been a dreadful summer, has it not?' she agreed. She was on firm ground here, having listened to Benedict talking over how best to save the crops on their estates and keep the tenants fed. 'Have your tenant farmers suffered?'

Edward looked startled. 'I have not heard of any distress.'

'Oh,' said Lilith, embarrassed. 'I daresay you have not had sufficient time yet to visit your farms and talk over their concerns.'

And now he looked uncomfortable. 'I . . . I don't, as a rule. Donald Kerr tells me what I need to know. He sees to the tenants.'

She hastily adjusted her ideas. 'He is your bailiff as well as secretary, then? You are fortunate. My brother's various agents would not let Benedict get away with such delegation.'

'It is lazy of me, I admit, but Kerr likes being in charge of the business.

He's far better at it than I am.'

'Naturally, that is his job. But how do you determine grievances if you are not familiar with the parties concerned? Whenever we travel to one of the estates, Ben is always shut up with his stewards for the first two days at least.'

'My father was the same, as is Henry. If I mention any such idea to Kerr, he becomes alarmingly stiff and Scottish and asks with painstaking politeness if I am perhaps not satisfied with his work? It would be like kicking a dog. This is a very small estate, after all.'

Good gracious, Edward Makepeace had a heart like honey. Who ever would have thought it?

'The sentiments do you credit,' said Lilith guardedly. 'It is not good practice though, not if your tenants are to respect you. However efficient and fair-minded Mr Kerr is, you would not have your people think you do not care?'

He regarded her with wry vexation.

'You have a most inconvenient conscience, Miss Fitzgilbert.'

'I have often found it annoying. It is why I am enjoying this visit to Newmarket so much — there is nothing for it to nag me with. Do you have arable farms or livestock here? If it is sheep, they will not be quite so affected by the wet.'

'Sheep. The wool revenues are down because of the weather.' He looked up at the sky and put his hat back on. 'And if I do not mistake the matter, there is another squall due shortly. Let us return to the house. Ricky can stride about the library declaiming in the warm and I will find you the treatise I have published on antiquarian practice.'

'I should like that very much.' But Lilith frowned to herself as she walked back to Ditton Place with the two brothers. She was not sure enough of her facts to argue, but she rather thought Ben's sheep were always shorn in the spring. The fleeces would not have been affected by the wet summer at all.

* ★ *

'Oh, this looks far better,' said Lilith to Hester, glancing around the library with approval. 'Did the maids say why they had not dusted ready for Mr Makepeace's arrival? It is evident this is the room the brothers use most often.'

'They're all new. They didn't know,' replied Hester succinctly with a look that indicated more would be forthcoming once they were alone.

Interesting. Lilith turned her attention to what Woods was telling Edward.

'Mr Atkins left before anyone was up this morning, sir. He was in a temper last night, by the sounds of it, so they stayed out of his way.'

'No doubt because I was about to turn him off,' said Edward cynically. 'I'd already had words with him about the condition of the house and the lack of servants. Then, when I was at Cheveley yesterday, I met a stable-hand who used to work for me. He'd been let go because he objected to Atkins interfering with the housemaid he was keeping company with. I taxed Atkins with this when we got back, he told me the man was a liar, I replied I wouldn't stand for any more, then Ricky and I retired for the night.'

Lilith shuddered. 'You are better off without him. He sounds thoroughly objectionable.'

'Indeed. Looks the part, but all words and no substance. I didn't expect him to run out on me without a proper severance, though. Devil take it, why did this have to happen now, just when I have scholars arriving?'

'I daresay you were the catalyst. There would be no need for him to abscond while you were absent.'

He looked at her, much struck. 'You're right. He had a comfortable roost here at my expense. I had better check to see whether I have any plate left.' He took a deep breath and addressed her frankly. 'I beg your pardon for not being able to offer you the hospitality due to you. A house in disorder must always reflect badly on the owner. Atkins also allowed my housekeeper to go on a visit to her sister last week — unless that was a lie too, and in reality she left months ago.'

'And the circumstances are going to tease you and prevent you working, and that annoys you.' Lilith gave him a smile. 'I understand. I told you in London that I expect no special treatment. I am very content to keep out of your way and read. Indeed, in such a library as this, I could sit and read forever.'

'You are kind to say so.'

'It is true. And let us not forget that you did not invite me, I invited myself. By way of reparation, can Woods or Hester be of any assistance in your preparations for the resident scholars?'

For a moment she thought he might refuse. She saw pride struggle with necessity in his face. Then he sighed and gave the fleeting smile that did wondrous things to his countenance. 'I would be very grateful. Kerr could not be absent at a worse time. What business he is transacting in Newmarket for this long, I cannot imagine. Ricky, can you . . . no, never mind. Kerr will come straight in here when he returns. You continue with your new epic. I will find you that volume on antiquarian practice, Miss Fitzgilbert.'

Lilith opened the first page thoughtfully. There was more than one puzzle here. The housekeeper had been gone well over a week. Edward might not realise it, but the level of dust indicated a month's lack of attention at least, and yet the underlying surfaces betokened good care previous to that.

Hester cleared her throat. 'There is a spare chamber upstairs where I can brush your skirts,' she said in a tone which didn't admit of argument.

Lilith rose obediently. 'How foresighted of you to have brought a brush,' she said with a sigh. 'Gentlemen, I shall return when Hester deems me suitable for company again.'

As she accompanied her hench-woman, she said mildly, 'You have made yourself at home, I see. Have you discovered why there is no house-keeper?'

'That I haven't. All the indoor servants were turned off at the same time several months ago, bar a couple of kitchen maids without the wit to think for themselves. The three maids working here now have only been in the place a sennight. Young Lucy said her mother wasn't very keen, on account of the butler having a reputation where girls are concerned — including Peter's older sister, who left of her own accord before the rest were let go. Lucy says she wasn't worried because her broth-ers would soon put Mr Atkins right if he tried anything, but as it happens he's been thick with Mrs Bell the cook — who is a most uncooperative woman — ever since Lucy got here and he hasn't bothered the maids at all.'

Hester commenced brushing down the hem of Lilith's gown. Lilith thought over what she had said. 'I wonder if Mr Makepeace is aware of all this. I do not think he can be, for he seems to leave a great deal to his secretary while he himself follows more scholarly pursuits. Perfect trust is a charming fault to have, of course, but it leaves him shockingly open to exploitation. The neglect is a shame, for this could be a lovely house, don't you think?'

'It's a handsome place, that's for sure. There. You'll do.'

Edward was waiting for them in the hall. 'Kerr has returned, so I have asked my coachman to wait and take you back. Your footman has collected your belongings and I have added my treatise to them. My apologies, but until I resolve this coil I cannot give my mind to earthworks and Romans, much as I should like to.'

He looked harassed. Lilith's sensibilities were touched. 'I understand. Perhaps you would give me your arm outside?'

He was clearly itching to be back in

his library thrashing out the problem of his missing butler, but he inclined his head politely. 'Certainly.'

As soon as she was sure they could not be overheard, she said in a low voice, 'You are wishing me gone, so I will say this quickly. Your servants were all turned off several months ago and the new ones engaged just last week. I suggest you now find that out for yourself. I am told your butler was very thick with your cook. From my own observation, your housekeeper left four or five weeks ago.'

Edward's mouth opened, then he snapped it shut. 'I am obliged to you,' he said, sounding anything but.

Hester hurried out with her pelisse, Lilith apologised for being so forgetful, and Woods opened the door of the carriage. Lilith saw him murmur a few words to Edward before saying 'Furze House in Newmarket,' cheerfully to the coachman and climbing up to sit next to him.

7

Ned stared after the departing carriage. Lilith's information sat uncompromisingly in his head, and now her footman was being elliptical. Something damned havey-cavey was going on here.

'Anything amiss, sir?' said Chilcott, who'd come out to take the horses but hadn't been required.

'Many things.' The servants leaving and not being replaced until a few days ago could be down to misplaced economy, but . . . 'Principally, I'd like to know why Miss Fitzgilbert's footman has just seen fit to inform me dinner at Furze House is at five, and Mrs Redding is a fine cook.'

Chilcott snorted. 'No mystery about that. He'll have passed through the kitchen here. Mrs Bell isn't taking Mr Atkins's defection too well. Five o'clock, you say? Very happy to accompany you over there to mind the horses.'

'You are an opportunistic rogue, Chilcott. I cannot go without an invitation from Miss Fitzgilbert. I have not been exactly welcoming today.'

'Mr Woods thinks you can, and he's a sensible sort of chap — for an indoor man, that is.'

'True.' He remembered something Lilith had said. 'And as I understand Furze House to be run on egalitarian principles, I can wear a comfortable coat rather than the hideous one Ferris will try to insert me into.' Much cheered, he returned to the library to tackle Kerr.

Ricky was at the table by the window, working on his verses. Kerr was standing in front of the fire with the air of one who has been told to wait, but whose time could be far better spent rectifying the situation than in the futile, blame-laying exercise he sensed was coming.

Ned ignored this subliminal message. What is the point of employing a secretary if you can't transfer your own feeling of inadequacy over to him? 'What do you know of the servant situation here?' *And why didn't you either tell me or do something about it?*

'As far as I was aware, all was in order. I had not been informed of any changes. The staff wages were paid on the quarter as usual. I drew it out and sent it to Mr Atkins as normal to pay it on.'

'He evidently *didn't* pass it on because three-quarters of the servants had been let go.'

Kerr pursed his lips. 'So it appears. I expressed my disappointment in the general level of service yesterday. He blamed Mrs Gunn's poor management of the maids.'

'There were no maids! Did he expect us not to notice the lack of servants? Mrs Gunn herself has been gone considerably more than a week. I should like to know why a valued housekeeper of long standing accepted her dismissal from a butler who has not been in the job a twelvemonth. Why did she not write to me? She cannot have thought I would be unconcerned.'

Kerr folded his hands. 'The letter may have gone astray. Atkins may have suppressed it. One cannot tell at this distance.'

'You had better request more staff from the registry office. If there are any of our former employees on their register, they must be given preference.'

Kerr pursed his lips. 'Is that wise? We do not know why Atkins let them go. It may be there was some dishonesty involved.'

'The only dishonesty was on Atkins's part,' snapped Ned. 'I want the whole house checked to see what else might be missing.'

His secretary stiffened with disapproval. 'Taking a full inventory will intrude considerably on the time I have available to do your own work, sir. Do not forget there is your important dinner coming up, and the arrangements for the Greek trip, should you raise the required funding.'

Ned's voice hardened. 'You suggest I let Atkins get away with theft?'

'Lodging information with the nearest magistrate and circulating a description of the man would be a sufficient measure. I can return to Newmarket and see to that now.'

'It must certainly be done without delay, but I also want an inventory taken,' repeated Ned. 'He has dismissed staff for no adequate reason and thus robbed them of their wages. It seems naive to assume he has not also stolen from me.'

He then strode crossly upstairs to despatch Ferris to the Three Blackbirds to enquire about Atkins, Mrs Gunn or the former servants. The sooner this house returned to normal the better.

Ferris took his task in much better part than Kerr had done. 'A sensible move, sir. A village landlord always has his finger on the pulse, so to speak. I'll drop in there this evening as soon as I've seen you off to Miss Fitzgilbert's house.'

Ned had long since ceased to be surprised by the way knowledge of his movements was transmitted instantaneously between the members of his personal retinue. 'I daresay you'll get more information out of him if you eat your meal at the Blackbirds at the same time.'

'It was in my mind,' said Ferris urbanely. 'Does Mr Richard accompany you to Furze House?'

'I asked him, but he says he'd prefer to use the evening to work on his new poem. He doesn't seem to mind Mrs Bell's cooking.'

'He has a happy nature, sir,' observed Ferris with feeling.

★ ★ ★

'Back again?' said a lean, dark gentleman who came strolling up from the stables as Chilcott opened the carriage door for Ned to alight. 'Can't keep you away.'

Ned was about to reply somewhat

tartly that this was his first visit to Furze House when he realised the gentleman was addressing his horses rather than himself. Also that he was a *gentleman*, despite his casual manner and attire.

'Good evening,' he said. 'I'm Edward Makepeace. I am aware this is highly irregular as I do not have an invitation, but earlier today Miss Fitzgilbert's footman informed me of the dinner hour here in such a way as to suggest I might find a welcome at your table. If I misunderstood him, I'll take myself off to one of the inns.'

'Ah, Lilith's antiquarian. She told us of your upsets. Nicholas Dacre. Welcome to Furze House.' He extended a hand for Ned to shake. His manner was affable, but in the lantern-lit shadows, Ned was aware of the man's watchful eyes assessing him.

'Pleased to meet you, Dacre. I've heard your name in town. Is this your house?'

'In a manner of speaking. Several of

us have an interest in Furze House. I am establishing a stable here so am in Newmarket most often. The outside staff refer to me as the guvnor, which would be more gratifying if I didn't suspect they principally wish to establish a line of command upwards in order to pass on problems. I'll let Catherine know there's one more place setting needed. Are your men staying?'

'That's very kind of you, sir,' put in Chilcott deferentially. 'We'll leave the horses here if we may, but the coachman and I thought we'd step up to the White Hart for a bite to eat. Maybe ask a few questions about missing butlers while we're there.'

'You can if you wish,' said Dacre, in an amused tone, 'but I think you'll find Molly Turner's been before you. She was off to the High Street as soon as Miss Fitzgilbert returned and told us why she was home early. She'll report back later.'

Ned chuckled at his groom's cha-grined expression. 'Fetch a jug of ale for the kitchen and take your meal in there if there's enough food to go around. Mr Dacre's groom will show you the way.' He turned back to Dacre. 'My thanks. I can't say I wasn't warned that Furze House was unorthodox.'

The other man grinned as he started towards the front of the house. 'It's all of that, and I won't deny it threw me at first. It's worse on the staff. My valet nearly gave notice on the spot when I told him there was no servants' hall. Sadly, he thought better of the impulse and has instead conjured up his nephew to be my 'country valet' as he terms it. Thank you, Woods. Show Mr Makepeace up, would you? I'll be with you once I've washed.'

After such a good-natured welcome, Ned was even more embarrassed at the abrupt way he had sent Lilith away from Ditton Place earlier. He was ushered into a handsome, first floor saloon with a good fire and the curtains drawn against the dusk. Lilith was seated at a table over which papers were spread, staring at them with a worried crease between her eyes. He was astonished to find his spirits lifting. He had spent less than a day with her, she had irritated him by meeting his fury over Atkins with calm good sense, she had shamed him by discovering facts about his household that he ought to have known months ago, and yet . . . and yet, mysteriously, she felt like a friend. For the first time in his life, he was pleased Ferris had persuaded him into a smarter waistcoat.

'Good evening,' he said awkwardly. 'I hope this is not an intrusion, but . . . '

She looked up. 'Hello,' she said, her face clearing. 'Have you come for your brother's poem? I do apologise: I did not realise I had brought it away with me. We were in such a hurry that everything got swept up together. I do not think it is the one he was telling me about, though, not the one he is working on now.'

Ned took the chair next to her and looked at Ricky's handwriting leaping energetically across the pages. 'That doesn't surprise me,' he said with fond exasperation. 'I doubt he even knows it is missing. He scatters pages of verse all over the house, scribbling on any spare paper he comes across. No blank surface is safe when he gets a fit of the muse. This page, for instance, is the back of a bill from my bootmaker for which I will doubtless be dunned, having not given it to Kerr to pay.'

She chuckled. A flicker of pleasure at having amused her licked through him.

'No,' he went on, 'I came because I have been making myself thoroughly unpopular at Ditton Place and could not face being resented on all sides whilst failing to eat an inedible meal. I also need to apologise for my excruciating manners this morning. Have you been trying to make sense of Ricky's stanzas? I wondered why you looked puzzled when I came in.'

'I have been reading them, yes. That was how I knew it was not his new epic. Parts are very good. He has a nice sense of rhythm. Other parts are . . . ' She broke off. 'Edward, what do you know about me, about my family?'

That you are direct, as I know to my cost. That you are intelligent. That I trust you. That I like the sound of my name on your lips. This last thought took him so much by surprise it temporarily robbed him of speech. 'Nothing. That is, I know you are interested in the arts. I know your stepmother holds regular soirées.'

She gave him a troubled look. 'My own small skill lies in drawing, but I have experience of all the creative disciplines. I have read a lot of poetry, good and bad. I have listened to much music, good and bad. I have viewed many paintings, also good and bad. I have met a wearisome number of people who are convinced they have the spark of greatness that will propel them to fame and riches.'

'Those would be at the soirées?'

He expected a rueful smile in response, but she remained serious.

'Edward, I have learnt to recognise when a person's natural ability has been . . . augmented.'

Ned stilled, all desire to tease her gone.

Lilith spread Ricky's pages in front of her, selected one particular sheet and held it. 'These verses here give every indication of having been written whilst your brother was taking laudanum. The images are terrible and beautiful. He has spears piercing rainbows and rivulets of vermilion and indigo coursing down the shaft. They are not in the same style as the other pages. I am sorry to grieve you, and if you say it is impossible I will be most thankful, but . . . '

He put his head in his hands. 'But you think it is true. Why do you tell me?'

'How could I not?'

He looked up again. *Direct and honest. She always would be.*

She continued. 'I tell you because he is your brother and you care for him.

Because he is very young — younger, I think, than his years. I know it is seen as fashionable amongst artists to use opium to unlock the muse, but the drug takes as well as gives. A few drops in a glass of wine to ease pain is acceptable. It is advocated by doctors. Prolonged use can be . . . unpredictable.'

There was pain and regret in her eyes. Ned found he had covered her hand with his own. 'I am so sorry. This happened to someone you knew? Someone you cared for?'

'A little, perhaps. He did not live long enough for us to find out.'

Ned cleared his throat. 'Ricky's . . . weakness is partly why we are here. Away from town, away from careless friends, away from apothecary's shops within two streets of the house. I thought to remove here last month, but there was the opportunity to give the lecture you came to, so we put it off. Ricky swears he has stopped. It has been very painful. It will be easier for him to keep to the resolution here.' He took a stinging breath. 'I suppose that particular page is not dated?'

Lilith looked at the sheet. 'Three weeks ago.'

Ned thought back. Around the time he had strong-armed his way into that filthy house in Wardour Street and slung Ricky over his shoulder to get him out. He breathed a sigh of relief that the verses had been written then and not later, indicating a broken promise to stay off the drug. 'Thank God. I know about that. Someone had persuaded him smoking the stuff produces the euphoria without the sickness and the craving for more. He won't say who it was. The man thought he was helping, apparently. If I ever find out his name, he will not need to worry about his own cravings, that's for sure.'

'Smoking?'

'It is done in the East, not here so much. A flame underneath the powder produces a vapour. Participants breath it in via a tube.'

'That sounds both uncomfortable

and insanitary,' said Lilith.

'It is a soporific. Ricky tells me the dreams are enchanting. From the reek of it in the house in Wardour Street where I found him, I'm not surprised nobody stopped me getting him out. They must have all been asleep themselves, servants and clients alike. Fortunately he weighs little, even as boneless as the session had left him, so I was able to carry him bodily out of the door and into a hackney. I apologise, Miss Fitzgilbert. I had no intention of burdening you with any of this.'

'You called me Lilith this morning. There is no need to apologise. If you had not known already, then I would have been burdening *you* with the news.'

Ned acknowledged this wryly. 'Your logic is irrefutable. Thank you. And thank you for mentioning it. Very few gentlemen of my acquaintance would have said anything, let alone ladies.'

Lilith smiled at him. 'You need better

friends. Of what use is experience, unless we use it to benefit others? Is there any news of your butler? Catherine's friend Molly has been to several hotels and not heard anything of him. She was going to try the others after her meal.'

Ned frowned. 'So Dacre said. Why would she do that? She does not even know me.'

Nicholas Dacre himself entered the room, freshly washed and changed. 'The women in this house are indefatigable, Makepeace. No sooner do they get a hint of some way in which they can help with a problem than there is no stopping them, whether they know the person concerned or not.'

Lilith gave him a speaking look. 'You have to admit, Nicholas, men will often let slip information to a lady that they would not mention to their own sex.'

'Undoubtedly,' he said, crossing to the decanter and pouring glasses of Madeira for them all. 'I am not complaining, Lilith. I am preparing our guest for the irrepressible nature of the Furze House females.'

Ned sipped the rich wine and found himself relaxing. 'I will accept all the help available. I have certainly learnt the lesson of being an absentee employer. I was too complacent and have been knocked down for my pains.'

'Can your previous butler help you out until someone suitable can be found?' asked Lilith. 'Where did he retire to?'

Ned felt a twinge of guilt. 'I don't know. He said he was making a home with his sister. Kerr dealt with it. Yes,' he added, forestalling her, 'you are quite right. I *should* know. *Mea culpa.*'

'Find the address from your secretary and write to him. It would be an advantage to have someone — even temporarily — who is accustomed to the workings of the house. When do your scholars arrive?'

'This week. I do not know exactly.' He saw the intelligent wrinkle appear on her brow again and hastened to explain. 'Spare me the scold I see forming, this is not more of my leaving things to other people. My friend Thornley is arranging the class. He already has his funding in place for the summer, so the men will be his team. He is taking over my Egyptian excavations.'

'I think I spoke to a Mr Thornley after your lecture. Sinfully good-looking, a lot to say for himself, but a sadly patronising attitude to female intelligence.'

'That sounds like Thornley, certainly. Did he offend you?' Ned was oddly pleased his famously seductive friend had not added Lilith to his list of admirers.

'He didn't mean to. He explained very carefully that the reason he took only gentlemen abroad on working parties was because the living conditions were primitive and the climate too harsh for delicate female complexions. I replied that in that case it was a wonder the Egyptian race had not died out entirely. I think he was not expecting to talk about the realities of child-bearing within the walls of Somerset House.'

Ned choked back a laugh. 'I daresay not. I wish I could have heard the exchange.'

'You were at the other end of the room being deferential to Lord Hazelmere.'

'Do not judge me too harshly for that. Lord Hazelmere is a great patron of the arts.'

'More money than sense, according to my grandfather,' put in Nicholas.

'Did he offer a subscription for your Greek trip?' asked Lilith.

'He is considering it. He will certainly be at the dinner I am giving. If I could only guarantee to find a set of marble carvings equivalent to those of Lord Elgin, I should probably never have to beg for funding again.'

'Now that does surprise me. From your treatise and your explanation this morning, I had not thought you interested in material gain.'

She had been reading his treatise. Ned beat down the pleasurable frisson the knowledge gave him. 'I am not. I am interested in the history, in the minutiae of ancient lives. Sadly, my backers do not have such highness of mind.'

He and Dacre stood as a second lady came in, laughing at someone outside. 'I came to let you know dinner is ready, but now I've offended Woods, so I've told him to give me half a minute and then announce it properly. I simply cannot get used to having a footman.'

Dacre reached out a hand to her and said, 'Your food is deserving of any number of announcements. Woods has the right of it entirely. May I introduce our guest Edward Makepeace? Edward, this is Mrs Catherine Redding, the lady of the house.'

She held out her hand, instantly hospitable. 'Lilith's antiquarian? I'm so pleased to meet you. You are welcome here any time. Do bring your brother if he would care to come.'

'Thank you,' said Ned, 'but that is a remarkably foolish suggestion. You will now never be able to get rid of us.'

From the doorway, Woods cleared his throat. 'Dinner is served.'

They moved towards the door, but the solemnity of the announcement was impaired by the wail of a baby from the landing above them, followed by a comely young lady hurtling down the stairs. She skidded to a halt at the turn, eyed Ned with the appreciative glance of a connoisseur and said to Catherine, 'Milk. Mrs S can't make enough and Hannah won't go for it, not with men in the house.' She then ran downwards towards, presumably, the kitchen. The wails from above grew louder.

'Our newest resident, making her feelings known,' said Catherine with a smile. 'Did Lilith tell you of Mrs Smith? I've put her next to Susan as Susan's own child is fifteen months old, so she can help look after her. Unfortunately one crying infant invariably sets off the other.'

Ned fell into step with Lilith. 'You did warn me,' he said. 'I now see what you mean about this house. Do I dare ask who Hannah is?'

'A very young maid who is scared of all men. Furze House is a refuge as well as a boarding house. Catherine is remarkable, taking them all in, but she says she likes the bustle and the feeling of life around her. It is very humbling. Do you see why I said I felt out of place?'

'Perfectly. Dacre tells me one gets used to it. Mrs Smith can count herself fortunate, I think. It is a shocking thing to be turned out so close to her time.'

'It is wicked. She is much too forgiving about it and is determined to pay her way here. She asked to do some mending, which is all she can manage at the moment. Catherine's friend Molly straightaway found her an old sheet to turn sides to middle, purely so she would feel useful. I am learning a lot from these women.'

And that made Lilith herself remarkable, reflected Ned. He could think of
no other ladies of his acquaintance who
would make the same admission.

8

Lilith watched Edward conversing easily with Nicholas at the dinner table. He was a man of many parts, acquitting himself as well in this semi-formal setting as he had behind the lectern at Somerset House. Walking to the Devil's Ditch, he had balanced into the wind as one born to it, yet his comfortable, book-filled library at Ditton Place clothed him like a second skin too.

'I congratulate you on the meal,' he said to Catherine. 'I feel able to deal with any number of reversals at home now.'

'It was delicious,' agreed Lilith. 'I am envious. I can plan for soirées, dinners and balls, but I am not the least use in the kitchen. And I shall never understand how a cook can miraculously produce a meal for three or four extra people on no notice, but they always do.'

Catherine chuckled, her eyes mischievous. 'I don't know how your chef in Bedford Square manages, but I learnt my cookery in an inn kitchen. I had best not tell you the stratagems employed there to feed an unknown quantity of hungry customers in double-quick time.'

'I am so glad you didn't raise that spectre *before* the meal,' said Nicholas.

Edward chuckled. 'In Egypt, the more people we had working on the site, the more rice-and mashed-bean-heavy our daily meals became. They were never boring though. Different spices were added to fool the palate into thinking we were eating quite different dishes.'

Catherine laughed. 'And there you have it, the cook's box of tricks laid bare for all to see. How very unhandsome of you, Mr Makepeace.'

'Please, won't you call me Edward or Ned? I feel so comfortable here, the formality makes me jump. Making a place feel like a home is evidently something else you have a talent for.'

A blush suffused Catherine's face. Nicholas kissed his hand to her. Lilith turned away at the love in his eyes, feeling as though she was intruding.

'I should be getting back shortly,' said Edward with some reluctance. 'Kerr will no doubt have a stack of letters for me to sign. Or else he will inform me reproachfully that there are no letters because he has been compiling the inventory of the house which I was so unreasonable as to ask for.' He met Lilith's eyes. 'And before you accuse me of ingratitude, I do know I am lucky to have him. He at least is worth his wages, unlike my butler who is a thieving rogue. This morning I was all for enquiring at every posting house and tracking Atkins down with vengeance in my heart. Now I am full of good food, mellowed by intelligent company and desire nothing more than a dish of tea and for my carriage to waft me home.'

Catherine rose. 'Take them upstairs, Lilith. I will fetch the tea and warn Edward's groom to be ready in twenty minutes.'

'I'll go out and do that,' said Nicholas. 'I need to stretch my legs.'

'I like your friends,' said Edward as he gave Lilith his arm up the staircase. It was not in the least necessary, but Lilith liked the unthinking courtesy and the feel of solid strength under her palm. 'If I do not raise the funds for Greece, it is good to know there are congenial souls in the neighbourhood where I can relax over the coming months.'

'But there can be no difficulty over that. Surely you must visit with several families in the area,' said Lilith, surprised.

'Ditton Place was my mother's property. We came for the racing, but my father preferred his own estates in Hampshire and Scotland the rest of the time. Since Mama died I have been in

Newmarket far more. As soon as I got Ricky into Westminster School, however, I felt obliged to stay in town during the terms in case he needed me. Additionally, a bachelor must steer a careful path when it comes to socialising, especially when his competence is not large and he has expensive interests.'

Was that a warning to her? Lilith felt herself colour. 'Why is your older brother not Ricky's guardian?'

'It made sense for me to assume responsibility. Ditton Place was left between me and Ricky. I have the management and two-thirds of the income, he has a third.'

'That does not seem very fair.'

'It does not bother me. Ricky would rather write than farm. He will need an income to sustain him. He has always been of a delicate constitution, so settled work is likely to be problematical. I promised Mama years ago I would look after him.'

And he was evidently a man who

stuck to his obligations. Lilith liked him all the more for it. 'Why have you not married?' she asked. 'Your wife could then share the charge.' *He was personable enough that he would have no trouble attracting applicants.*

She almost laughed aloud at the dismay on his face. 'Have you any idea how much time and effort goes into identifying and courting a suitable bride? I would never get any of my own work done at all.'

'Oh, you men! You sound just like Benedict. Can you not see that after the thing is done, you would be vastly more comfortable and never have to worry about it again?'

He looked disbelieving. 'The endeavour is immense. So much to consider. My father was brokering a suitable alliance for me, but at the house party where I was supposed to offer for her, he had a seizure and died.'

'Oh good heavens!' said Lilith, shocked.

'Indeed. He was waiting for the hunt

141

to start, surrounded by members of the ton, when he grunted and toppled from his horse. Naturally it would have been impossible for me to continue with the offer. As neither of our affections were engaged, the most delicate course was to say nothing to either the lady concerned or her father. I fancy they were both pleased at my restraint.'

Lilith kept her own council. The father might have been appreciative of Edward's thoughtfulness, but she couldn't imagine the lady viewing the loss of such a splendid example of English manhood with any degree of complaisance. 'Shall I come to Ditton Place tomorrow?' she asked, changing the subject. 'Will you have time to teach me what it is you do?'

'Yes, certainly. You have made a start on the method already, and I will get the records out so you can see the conclusions I have drawn so far. One of the blessings of Ditton Place being mine is that I have been able to build up the library. The town house belongs to Henry, though we all reside there when we are up. I am guilty of staying far longer than I should, simply because London is so convenient for everything.'

Lilith laughed. 'It is, isn't it? There is always a reason to stay one more week, or to put off a journey by a couple of days. Yet now I am revelling in the freedom to do as I please. Does one ever lose the desire to learn, do you suppose? I feel as though I could never have enough of it. It may be different for men, but it is a treat for me not to have to organise the daily round of life in a large house. I can give myself up to the acquiring of knowledge.'

'That I understand perfectly,' he said. 'I shall try to find enough for you to do. I confess, this is in part why I do not begrudge Donald Kerr's salary. He deals with the chores whilst I immerse myself in interesting bits of history.'

'Even though it is not lucrative?'

'It loses money faster than a storm drain gushes water, but we *have* to learn from the past. If we did not, every man would waste half his life discovering his craft anew. Mr Nash, for instance, would not be able to design his houses better than the architect before him. Chippendale or Hepplewhite would still be hollowing canoes out of fallen trees instead of making beautiful furniture. Weston would be dressing us in doublet and hose. Hoby would have us all wear clogs. Civilisation must move on, but we do it better if we build on the solid foundations of the past.'

He believed every word. That was what made him such a charismatic speaker. Lilith found her heart beating faster at the passion in his words. 'You must remember that phrase for when you deliver the speech at your dinner,' she said lightly.

He gave a short laugh. 'It will make little difference. They are interested in investments, not principles.'

'Some may be more open-minded than you think, especially when you couch it like that, in sentiments they can relate to. Talking of Mr Nash, what do you think of his new London development? It will be grand indeed when it is finished, very classical in style. But oh, the noise and dust and confusion every time we venture down the street.'

'Dreadful, isn't it,' agreed Nicholas, coming in and dropping casually into a chair. He was followed by Woods and the tea tray. There was nothing special in his manner, but Lilith thought he was alert to a high degree when he said, 'It seems Nash is experiencing problems with his builders. One man was threatened with disruption to his supplies unless he paid a certain amount over and above the price of the goods. He didn't pay and was found in the Thames.'

Edward's face darkened. 'That's despicable. I cannot abide bullies.'

'No indeed. I understand all those working for Nash are now under orders to report any such attempts directly to him.'

Edward nodded. 'Open forums have many merits. The Romans used them. If there is no secrecy, it makes it harder for bullies to flourish.' He smiled ruefully. 'This is why I like my work with the past. I can strip off a layer of soil and record what lies underneath and never worry about day-to-day problems.'

He drank his tea and left, after repeating his thanks to Catherine for the meal.

Lilith fixed Nicholas with a glance. 'Why did you mention Nash's troubles?'

'I was judging his reactions,' he replied bluntly. 'We know Nash's builders are being threatened by Flint. I wanted to make quite sure we weren't inadvertently harbouring one of his agents. Flint is still after Catherine, don't forget. He knows of her connection to this part of the world, and she is a danger to him. While he thinks there is the slightest chance she could identify him, she is not safe.'

Lilith felt shock run right through

her. 'Nicholas! You *cannot* think Edward has anything to do with Flint!'

'Flint has contacts everywhere, Lilith. This was a precaution. I do not believe Ned Makepeace is part of his network, but where Catherine's safety is concerned, I am never going to be complacent. Flint has sent one man to Newmarket already to nose her out. He could send another. The Pool's strength lies in staying hidden and remaining watchful.'

'But you were talking to Edward, laughing with him . . . '

'I like him. I would like not to mind my tongue around him. For your sake, I would like to know I can trust him. And he *was* seen coming out of a house in Wardour Street which we know Flint has an interest in.'

'Wardour Street?' said Lilith quickly. 'Is that the one where visitors smoke opium? Edward mentioned it to me earlier. He was rescuing his brother. An acquaintance had persuaded Ricky in there. Edward was furious about it.'

Nicholas's gaze sharpened. 'Yes,

that's the one. Which acquaintance?'

She shook her head. 'Ricky won't tell him. I apologise, I should not have been so quick to fire up at you.'

He subsided with a sigh. 'It is always the way. A promising lead and a dead end. If you do find out, let me know.'

Later, in her own chamber as Hester moved around laying out nightclothes, unpinning her hair and brushing it, Lilith thought about the swift course of anger that had flowed through her when Edward had been doubted. In her own mind she was quite certain Edward was exactly what he seemed, but Nicholas was right that they hardly knew him. It would do no harm to guard herself in their future dealings. The fact that the thought filled her with no pleasure should not be allowed to weigh with her at all.

* * *

On his return to Ditton Place, Ned found, as he had expected, Ricky still working on his poem in the library. 'Miss Fitzgilbert apologises, but she carried these off by mistake,' he said, giving him Lilith's pages. He badly wanted to mention the laudanum-inspired sheet, but restrained himself. Ricky had given his word to stop. Ned had to be seen to trust him. But it was hard. 'She said she enjoyed them very much. Why have you let the fire get so low? You will be catching a chill.' He crossed to the grate and placed another log on the burning embers.

'I was warm enough,' said Ricky. 'Did she really like them? Is she coming tomorrow? She can see the rest if she is minded to.'

'She is joining the excavation in order to learn about unlocking history,' Ned replied. 'That is what she is paying me for, so do try not to monopolise her. Ricky, you are cold. You should have a hot drink.' He strode to the door and asked the young footman in the hall to bring in the tea tray.

No soon had he made the request

than Kerr came down the stairs, a sheaf of letters in his hand. 'I thought I heard you return. These all require your signature.'

Ned braced himself to deal with his secretary's passive superiority. It was the price he paid for the freedom to devote himself to his work, but it was irritating nevertheless. 'Bring them in then. What are they?'

'Requests for investments. Applications to the Greek authorities. I have also taken an inventory of the dining room and the saloon as being the areas Mr Atkins was most concerned with. I am told several chambers have been prepared for the scholars, should they arrive tomorrow.'

'Thank you. I hope the weather will not prove an obstacle. The wind is increasing and it was already raining as we came back from Newmarket. Chilcott, however, is of the opinion it will blow itself out towards morning and dry up.'

'That will certainly be more convenient for your excavation,' said Kerr, gathering up each letter as it was signed and laying the next one down in its place.

Ned remembered Lilith's suggestion from earlier. 'Would Locke come back to us temporarily if there is no other butler suitable? Where does he live now?'

'I doubt he would be up to the work. I understand he is in poor health.'

Ned looked up, mortified. 'And you didn't mention it to me? Locke is a very old retainer. I should send a note of sympathy. I will write one tonight.' *And now Kerr will be even more silently reproving, first because I disappeared for the evening while he worked, and second because I have criticised him.*

Kerr was indeed so reproachful that he withdrew without another word. Ned reminded himself that he, not his secretary, was master here, and dashed off a courteous note to Locke for Kerr to address and mail. He then drank his tea with Ricky and continued to unpack the crates he had been dispatching here since the spring. Passing the chair Lilith had been curled up in earlier, he smiled, but when Ricky asked what was amusing him he was hard-pressed to know. The closest he could come to it was that she had not been as unreasonable as he'd been expecting and that she'd turned a ghastly muddle into a normal working day. Certainly he had enjoyed talking to her this evening. It would be no hardship to teach her the basics of antiquarian practice.

Insulated from the gale blowing outside, it was pleasant putting books and curios on the shelves, remembering where he had acquired them, listening to the scratch of Ricky's pen and occasionally giving his opinion on a verse or a phrase. So pleasant that it was quite late when they doused the candles. In the hall, the young footman was dozing. Ned felt a pang of guilt. 'Have we made you late?' he said. 'I should have said you could retire once you had brought the tea tray in.'

'I'm all right, sir. Mr Kerr's been

down once or twice, but he didn't want nothing. Mr Woods told me it was all bobbin to sit in a chair to wait. He's a great gun, is Mr Woods. He's learnt me more today than Mr Atkins did all week. I've locked up, so it won't take a trice until I'm between my sheets. You've no need to worry about housebreakers neither. I'll sleep with the keys under my pillow.'

He was so earnest and willing to please that Ned nodded gravely. 'Very good. I can see you are going to be a valuable addition to the household.'

As he and Ricky reached the bedroom landing, Kerr emerged from his study. 'If you are thinking of going for an evening stroll, you're too late,' said Ned. 'Everything is locked up.'

His secretary adopted the strained visage of one whose employer is lamentably prone to drollery. 'I was going to enquire if you needed anything more tonight. As you evidently don't, I will retire.'

Ned sighed. 'So many words,' he

murmured to the closed door. 'Goodnight, Ricky. Go to bed, now. Don't sit up.'

'To bed,' replied Ricky, 'perforce to dream.' He grinned suddenly. 'Or not. Goodnight, Ned.'

9

Ned was woken by at least one flash of lightning during the night and a distant crash. *Tree,* supplied his subconscious, and he went back to sleep.

The morning brought weak sunshine and Ferris with the intelligence that whatever else might be lacking in the house, logs for the fires were unlikely to be in short supply for the next few weeks.

'That bad, eh?' said Ned, grimacing. 'I'll take a look as soon as I'm dressed.'

There were leaves and branches strewn across the lawns on one side of the house, indicating that the wood near the beginning of the Devil's Ditch had born the brunt of last night's weather. Ned kicked the branches away from the drive and had started to cross to the wood when he heard the rumble of wheels and the clopping of hooves.

155

Baker's cart, he thought to himself, but shading his eyes against the low sun, he saw to his surprise that a modest carriage approached.

Lilith's footman Woods descended from the seat by the driver and opened the door. Ned hastily moved forward to hand down the occupant.

'I know, I know, we are shockingly early,' said Lilith cheerfully. 'But we have good reasons, so I am sure you will forgive us when you know.'

Ned discovered he was still holding her hand. He also discovered he quite liked it. 'You can never be too early,' he said, smiling, 'but I hope you have already breakfasted, for the food here will be a sad disappointment after Furze House. I had just made up my mind to rob the baker's cart on its way to the kitchen.'

'My dear sir, we have all been up for so long that breakfast is very nearly a distant memory,' said Lilith. 'Mrs Smith's baby, let me tell you, is the loudest creature in creation. Ma Turner

156

is of the opinion that the child is fretful because her mother is so morbidly anxious about her future that she is in some way communicating her worry. I said to immediately convey a personal promise of employment from me, purely in order to obtain a night's sleep.'

Ned laughed and offered his arm. 'It is more likely to have been the storm that disturbed the child. I was about to take a survey of the damage to the home wood. Do you care to join me?'

She smiled up into his face. 'Certainly, but I think Hester would rather go inside to stir up your maids. Woods can loiter at a discreet distance behind us in case you require him to move fallen trees out of our path.'

'I believe climbing over them might be easier,' said Ned with a straight face.

'Really? He is very resourceful.' She chuckled at the absurdity of their banter. 'My other news and the reason for being here early is that your scholars have arrived in Newmarket. Mr Grimes here is to bring them along after they have breakfasted and paid their shot at the White Hart.' She indicated the shabby carriage. The driver doffed his cap to him.

Ned's spirits lifted still further. 'You are a fund of unexpected knowledge today. I forgive you for not being the baker's cart. I am now waiting with bated breath to discover how it comes about that you are so cognisant of my affairs?'

Her grey-green eyes twinkled in the pale sunshine. 'The advantages of a small town and an unconventional household. While we were enjoying our meal last night, Molly Turner was in the White Hart drumming up business for their laundry — at least, I assume that's what she meant by 'looking for work' — where she made the acquaintance of a party of young gentlemen newly arrived from London and enquiring about conveyances to Ditton Place on the morrow. She immediately undertook to book Mr Grimes's carriage for them at a modest price. Catherine is of the belief that she also hired herself to the gentleman in charge of the scholars for not quite such a modest price. And presumably not for laundry work either.'

'What, is Thornley here too?' cried Ned. *If so, it would definitely not have been laundry under discussion.*

'Somebody certainly was. I must say, my experience of life is being expanded enormously. I am more than ever glad I . . . swapped town for country.'

Ned noticed her hesitation, but he was distracted by the news of Thornley. He didn't make the mistake of thinking his friend was here for the Cambridgeshire air. Either he was being dunned by his tailor or pursued by the menfolk of a beautiful, but misguided, young woman. He had best make the most of Lilith's company while he had her to himself. Thornley could no more ignore a handsome female than he could fly.

'I am always glad to see my friends,' he said now, 'but Thornley could not have chosen a worse time to visit with the management of the household in such disarray. Even if Kerr has luck at the registry for the general staff, there is unlikely to be a butler or a housekeeper available to start straight away.'

'And if they are, you would wonder why,' agreed Lilith. She glanced up at him with the sort of speculation that immediately made him uneasy. 'What are your feelings on children?'

'As a species or in particular? I liked Ricky when he was young. My brother's children, on the other hand, are only tolerable in very small doses. I am definitely not employing a child as a butler.'

She shook his arm gently. 'Foolish man. I told you I vowed to employ Mrs Smith myself if it would allay her anxiety enough to stop her daughter crying. It now occurs to me that she might be the very person to be your new housekeeper, but only if you had no objection to her bringing the babe with her.'

He regarded her with a humorous twist to his mouth. 'That is extraordinarily magnanimous of you. You are confident that I will not mind being woken up several times in the night?'

'I cannot believe a house this size and of this antiquity will not have a housekeeper's suite tucked away somewhere. I doubt you will hear a thing.'

'I should prefer to know more of this Mrs Smith first. Where she was before. How long she had been there. You know the sort of things I should ask her far better than I. Can you enquire for me? Careful now, the ground is beginning to be uneven.' Not only uneven, but littered with brush and branches. The familiar path through the wood was a good deal more challenging than usual.

'Your groundsmen will be busy for several days,' observed Lilith as they skirted a fallen tree trunk.

'Yes, I heard at least one crash last night. I daresay there may be more. As well that I had already decided the working at this end of the dyke should be abandoned. It is likely to be even more unstable now.' He paused, his eyes sharpening. There looked to be a bundle lying on the ground a little further on. A bundle that seemed to be . . .

He halted, automatically moving to shield Lilith. 'Woods,' he called. 'I need your help here.'

'What is it?' asked Lilith, then drew a sharp breath. 'Edward! Is that a person on the ground?'

'It is,' said Ned. 'Stay here.' He trod hurriedly over the layer of broken branches to get to the fallen man and tried to recall the names of his outdoor staff, for it must surely be one of them, come out to see the damage and been caught unawares. He reached for the man's shoulder.

'Kerr!' he exclaimed in shock. He sat back on his heels, utterly astounded. His secretary was the last person he would expect to find face down in mud and leaf litter in his wood. There was blood congealing on his temple. The man himself was immobile.

Woods hastened to his side and dropped to his haunches. 'He's breathing, sir. We might get him to the house between us if I take his shoulders and you support his legs.'

'He needs a doctor,' said Lilith, coming up to them despite Ned's direction to stay where she was. 'Careful, Woods. Do not . . . oh, too late.'

The sudden movement had brought Kerr to consciousness. He gave a gasping groan and cast up his accounts, narrowly missing Ned's feet.

'What happened, Kerr? What were you doing outside at this hour?' asked Ned.

His secretary's gaze glanced off him, uncomprehending. He put down a shaky hand to push himself vertical and instantly screamed with pain.

'Broken leg?' suggested Woods. 'I'd best fetch young Peter and a tabletop to carry him into the house.'

'Broken leg or broken head. Go to the stable first and ask Chilcott to send to Newmarket for the doctor,' said Ned.

Woods nodded and strode off. Ned scanned the ground. 'Kerr must have mistaken his footing and hit his head on the stump of this oak. It is an old felling, but last night's storm has bought brash down on top of it. See, there is a concealed branch here, half-hidden in the leaf litter. If the gardeners had not been so reduced by that scoundrel of a butler, it would have been cleared before now.'

'He is very cold,' murmured Lilith. 'He must have been out here some time. Was he accustomed to take early-morning constitutionals?'

'He is extremely fit and walks a great deal as a matter of course, but as to dawn strolls? He has never mentioned such a thing. He keeps himself to himself.' Ned was obscurely annoyed by his lack of knowledge. He suspected

Lilith knew the habits of all her household, whether it was volunteered or not.

Kerr had lapsed back into unconsciousness. Probably as well.

'I'm sorry,' he said. 'This is yet another disastrous welcome to Ditton Place. You will be getting a dislike of the place.'

'Unconventional, but not especially off-putting,' replied Lilith. 'Certainly not disastrous.'

'You are very kind.' A crashing amongst the undergrowth brought a useful distraction. 'Here are the footmen. Your man Woods is efficiency personified.'

Kerr screamed again as they got him on to the upturned table and started to carry him back to the house.

'Front parlour,' said Ned tersely. The table was heavy and Kerr was not a light man. Lilith walked briskly ahead to hold doors open. She had evidently been doing some thinking of her own whilst listening to Kerr's screams.

'Laudanum,' she said to Ricky. 'Quickly.'

Ricky turned and ran upstairs. Ned praised her forethought, but felt his heart sink as his brother hurried back down with a large bottle.

'It's all right, Ned, I haven't used any,' he said. 'See? It's full. I haven't broken my promise. It's just . . . comforting to know it's there.'

Ned gave his brother's arm a squeeze. 'I didn't doubt you,' he said gruffly and shook the bottle. 'Take some of this, Kerr. It'll ease the pain until the doctor gets here and sets your leg.'

His secretary's eyes widened in horror as Ned advanced. 'No,' he said. 'No.'

Then he shouted again as Lilith accidentally knocked his ankle and Ned tipped a good slug of the liquid down his throat.

'That worked,' she observed. 'Though usually one would add it to a glass of cordial or wine first.'

Ned tried to hide his grin as he met her eyes, and failed.

There was a commotion at the door. Woods reported that the doctor was approaching, followed by Mr Grimes with the scholars.

Naturally everyone would arrive together. It needed only that to complete Ned's portrayal of inefficiency. He refrained from clutching at his hair. 'The doctor takes precedence,' he said. 'Show the others into the library and provide a jug of ale. Say I'll be with them presently.'

'Or you could greet them yourself,' suggested Lilith. 'Hester and I are perfectly capable of attending Mr Kerr while the doctor examines him.'

Ned looked at her irresolutely for a moment, then nodded. 'Thank you. Forgive me, I am not accustomed to . . .'

'Letting other people do the thinking?' said Lilith with a twinkle in her eye.

Having someone to help me. 'That

too,' he replied, and went outside.

Fred Grimes grinned at him amiably. 'Lively party of gents here,' he said, with a backwards jerk of his thumb to the young men squeezing out of the carriage. 'I'll go back for their baggage as soon as they've tipped me the fare.'

'Make sure you get it in advance,' advised Ned. 'They'll plead poverty as soon as look at you.'

'Don't you worry about me, sir. I've driven a hackney in London for near on fifteen years. Up to all the tricks, I am.'

While the young gentlemen settled up with Grimes, Ned greeted the doctor and passed him to Woods to usher into the parlour. Peter, copying his mentor faithfully, led the scholars inside. Ned was about to follow them when a sporting curricle trotted up the drive with Thornley handling the reins in a negligently accomplished fashion.

'This is an unexpected pleasure,' remarked Ned. 'Is there some reason why I am blessed with your presence?'

'So welcoming always, dear boy. I'm averting disaster. My maternal aunt and appallingly plain cousin are in town for a week. They expected me to squire them to some dull dinner tonight and dance attendance on them for the length of their visit. I remembered you in the nick of time and said I was desolated, but I was bringing my class up here. Couldn't let you down. Nothing to be done.'

'Thornley, I'm touched.'

'So is my aunt. Fortunately they have an engagement at home a week today, so London will be safe again.'

'You'll be glad to go by then. The food here is terrible.'

Thornley's face shone with innocence. 'No, no, I wouldn't dream of asking you to feed me. I shall take myself into Newmarket in the evenings. Renew my acquaintance with the very pleasant armful I met yesterday.'

Definitely not laundry. Ned inclined his head. 'An admirable plan. Shall we

169

go in? I'll do the site introduction and run through the finer points of note-taking.'

He had got as far as explaining that he was using the Colt Hoare systematic approach as any finds were likely to be quite small in nature — this eminent gentleman, as he was sure the scholars already knew, being the excavator of the ancient stone circle at Stonehenge in Wiltshire — when he saw Lilith slip through the door.

'Doctor,' she mouthed.

He nodded, wound up what he was saying and excused himself, saying he would be back shortly.

The doctor remarked disapprovingly that his patient shouldn't have been moved until he'd got there, but reluctantly agreed no further harm appeared to have been done.

'There's no break that I can discover, so it is likely to be a bad sprain and possibly the muscle in the leg is torn. I've immobilised it so he doesn't try walking. His head is a good deal shaken up, as must be expected. He needs to be kept quiet, in a darkened room, and dosed regularly with the laudanum for now. I've given Miss Fitzgilbert instructions regarding nourishment and I'll call back tomorrow to see how he gets on. Have you the men to carry him prone to his bed?'

Ned assured him that all would be done, saw him out to his carriage and returned to the library. His mind was wholly on asking Lilith about the doctor's instructions. He wasn't at all prepared for the disagreeable sensation that ran through him on seeing her in animated conversation with Thornley.

She brought the dialogue to a laughing close and turned to ask if Ned required her help in organising Kerr's removal to his own bedchamber.

'Both footmen, together with Ricky and I, can move him, I think,' he replied. Then, seeing his friend waiting to resume the conversation, he added basely, 'Will you come and explain to Ferris what is required in terms of nourishment? He can set it in train with the kitchen.'

* * *

'We are busier here than we are at home,' muttered Lilith to Hester as they followed the group bearing Edward's secretary upstairs. *And just as little achieved to the purpose.* She stifled an unworthy pang at the thought of all those lovely books in the library waiting to be read. Duty must always come first.

The secretary's bedchamber was as austere as his connecting study. Mr Kerr seemed devoid of personality. 'I feel I should warn you I am not the least use in a sick room,' she said to Edward.

'Good God, I am not expecting you to be,' he replied, looking revolted. 'Ferris will deal with all that. If you convey the doctor's instructions to him, we can see Kerr settled and then get outside to the site. Now the men are here, I'd rather they were working on my Ditch than drinking my ale.' An arrested look came into his eyes. 'Unless you would prefer to continue with some reading in the library? I will largely be going over what I told you yesterday and explaining to Thornley my findings so far. It seems nonsensical for you and your maid to stand around in the cold. Ricky will no doubt remain inside with you.'

She beamed at him. 'That sounds *very* agreeable. I have been longing to get in amongst your books all morning.'

A gentleman's gentleman entered the room, evidently Ferris. 'Mr Kerr is principally to be kept as still as possible,' she told him. 'The doctor isn't happy that he appears to be in so much pain from a simple sprain. He couldn't even tell us what happened without screaming in agony. The doctor is worried there might be complications that will hamper recovery. Keeping him asleep while everything mends is a sensible precaution, he thinks. Dose with laudanum when necessary, otherwise lemon barley, a sustaining broth, and thin gruel once he is conscious enough to take solid food.' She glanced at Hester. 'Have I forgotten anything?'

Hester shook her head. 'That was it, and I wish you luck procuring a nourishing broth out of that kitchen, Mr Ferris.'

The valet, a capable looking man of middling years, shrugged. 'I shall have a word with Mrs Bell. The incident sounds much the same as when Master Richard fell out of the apple tree that time. Bent his leg sideways and shook his head up something shocking. Always a terribly restive patient was Master Richard.'

'Ferris!' objected Ricky, colouring.

The valet continued. 'As for the kitchen, it's inducing Mrs Bell to stop boiling when a dish is done that's the trick. Mrs Gunn had the art of it, as I recall. Only plain fare ordered, and she kept an eye on it herself.'

'I wish Mrs Gunn was back here

now,' said Edward with feeling. 'Has no one discovered anything about her in the village?'

'The villagers aren't talking.'

Edward grimaced. 'Which isn't the same as there being nothing to say. Something must have happened that she would leave without a word to me. Perhaps if news gets out that Atkins has gone, she might come back?'

'It is a possibility, sir, though she will likely have a position somewhere else by now.'

'True,' said Edward glumly. 'Heigh ho. I must get my party to the Ditch before they drink the barrel dry. Do make free of the library when you are ready, Miss Fitzgilbert.'

He hurried out, taking Ricky with him.

Ferris cleared his throat. 'If you could just watch Mr Kerr, miss, while I have a discussion with Mrs Bell regarding lemon barley. I should not keep you long.'

More delays. Lilith regarded the bed

where the patient was muttering and shifting restlessly. 'You had best remain also, Woods.' She moved closer to listen, but shook her head in frustration. 'There are no words in this. No explanation. Mr Makepeace is very likely correct that he tripped on a fallen branch, turned his ankle and hit his head. Does he need more laudanum, Hester? The doctor said we might give him a little extra if he didn't quieten.'

'It might calm him,' agreed her henchwoman. She pinched Kerr's nose and induced him to swallow another spoonful. 'It'll be bitter, but will work faster than mixing it.'

Lilith studied the secretary. Had he been at that lecture? He had a colourless, forgettable face that would blend easily into a sea of others. Unlike Mr Thornley. He had recognised her with flattering alacrity and had been telling her about Egypt, how civilised it was and how he was looking forward to the summer, being able to hire porters for pennies to do all the fetching and carrying and making the camp.

'Quite ridiculously cheap,' he'd said. 'One wonders how they manage to live.'

He hadn't looked particularly concerned. She imagined if the same point was raised with Edward, a furrow of worry would appear on his brow and he'd double the porters' wages whether he could afford it or not.

The mutterings from the bed grew louder. Woods trod swiftly across to hold Kerr down as he started threshing about. Hester armed herself with the bottle of laudanum again, ready to administer more.

'Mrs Eastwick,' gasped Kerr, shockingly clear despite his rasping breath. His eyes were wide open and fixed unseeingly on the ceiling. 'Must find Mrs Eastwick. Not at church. Must send word.'

Mrs Eastwick? A fist clutched at Lilith's heart. She heard herself gasp. Eastwick was Catherine's real name. Her husband had been of one of Flint's lieutenants, killed on his orders. Catherine had fled from London with Nicholas Dacre and forged a new identity as Mrs Redding. There was only one reason anybody would be looking for her. Flint wanted her dead.

'Send word to who?' she asked urgently, but the secretary had fallen back on to the pillows and his muttering had subsided. The laudanum was taking effect.

Lilith could have screamed with frustration. 'The poor man,' she said shakily aloud. 'He must have hit his head harder than we realised. He is not making any sense.'

Hester met her gaze steadily. 'None,' she agreed.

'Addled,' said Woods. 'That's what he is. Addled.'

10

Ned was ruthless in sweeping Thornley outside along with his class. In vain did his friend protest that he'd seen the damn ridge, thank you, and he was already well acquainted with the vallum-and-fosse and all Ned's theories about its construction. Ned retorted that studying it again was a small price to pay for avoiding his aunt. For himself, parrying Thornley's bitter complaints (*'Wet, slippery and cold, damn you'*) was a small price to pay for curtailing his friend's opportunity to forge a better acquaintance with Lilith Fitzgilbert. It wasn't that he didn't think she could cope. He simply didn't see why she should have to when she was here to study.

This noble thought sustained him until he remembered her carriage would be returning to collect her at three o'clock, so if he wanted to have any more speech with her himself, he had best be indoors before then.

'Can we walk along the top?' asked one of the young men.

'Certainly. There are steps cut at the end, but the site is unstable, so you'll need to take care when descending. My secretary is already laid up. I'd rather not add to the tally.'

He and Thornley strolled back alongside the dyke. The scholars elected to stride along the top.

'So,' said Thornley, 'Miss Fitzgilbert . . . '

'Is here for a course of private instruction into the study of antiquities and antiquarian methods.'

'Oh, well done,' said Thornley appreciatively. 'You do know she is Lord Fitzgilbert's sister?'

'I have given Lord Fitzgilbert my word that she will be entirely safe while under my roof. And before you ask, she is staying with friends and only visiting Ditton Place during the day.'

180

What Thornley would have replied to this, they were destined never to know. They had reached the end of the dyke. Above them, the good-natured banter from the top of the ridge changed suddenly to alarm.

'Mr Makepeace! Mr Thornley! There's somebody down there. There's someone in the ditch.'

Ned scrambled up the turf steps at a run. Looking down to where the men were pointing, he caught his breath. It was twenty-five feet to ground level. Fifteen feet below that, at the bottom of the ditch and looking curiously fore-shortened, lay the outflung body of his butler. His hat had fallen from his head. Two valises were tumbled next to him, one spilling its contents. It was clear Atkins hadn't moved for some considerable time.

The day slowed to a standstill. Through his strong horror, Ned was aware of everything. Of the wind. Of the distant cracks of a shooting party. Of his own heartbeat. 'Thornley,' he called down, surprised to hear his voice so steady, 'can you go to the stables and find Chilcott? Tell him I need planks and ropes.' To the men on the ridge, he said, 'Anyone who wishes to return to the house, please do. I have to go around to the far side of the dyke and drop into the ditch.' Then he turned, feeling very carefully for each handhold as he descended.

Chilcott, arriving on the ditch side with a couple of stable hands, was unflappable and matter of fact. 'I doubt there's any hope of life if he's been there two nights, but you'll be wanting to check,' he said. 'I've brought the long ladder. I'll steady the top.'

As he climbed down, Ned had another moment of horrified clarity. Atkins must have been lying here when he and Lilith had passed by on the other side yesterday. Might there have been a chance of saving him if he'd suggested they look at the start of the dyke then?

There wasn't any chance now. A

single brief touch with the back of his hand on Atkins's cheek confirmed it. The body was ice-cold and wet through. Thief or not, slow exposure was a dreadful death for anyone. Past memories scoured through his mind. Looking for Ricky in a blizzard. Finding his mother instead. He straightened up, unable to think through his nausea. Should Atkins be hauled out and laid decently to rest in a barn? Or was it better to cover him and leave him here for now? Who was the local JP? Who was he going to send to explain, with Kerr laid up?

'The doctor will know the procedure,' said Chilcott from the top of the ditch. 'I'll go into town again once you're out of there.'

Of course. That was the immediate solution. Thank heavens for Chilcott's steady sense. Ned collected Atkins's scattered belongings. His dependents, if there were any, could at least have these. 'He must have missed his way in the dark,' he said soberly. 'Heading for the lane to Dullingham and then the London Road.' Had Kerr discovered him this morning and been hurrying back to the house to raise the alarm? It would explain why he hadn't been looking where he was going. Though why his secretary would be heading for the Dullingham lane was another puzzle.

★　★　★

When the scholars burst into the library talking of dead men in ditches, Lilith gasped in alarm. Not Edward, surely? She and Ricky both pushed their chairs back and stood, not knowing what to do next.

'A vagrant?' wondered Ricky uncertainly.

'Your brother will tell us when he returns,' said Lilith. She gathered her scattered wits and suggested he take the budding antiquarians up to the rooms that had been prepared for them. Their luggage had arrived while they were out and was waiting to be carried up.

Edward and Mr Thornley came in together. 'We have found Atkins,' said Edward, coming straight across to her. 'He must have been taking a shortcut to the lane, and fell into the ditch in error. Chilcott has gone for the authorities. I regret I am going to be unable to devote any further time to your instruction today.'

He looked strained and worried. Lilith pushed away her concerns regarding Donald Kerr's cryptic utterances — and how she could prevent him repeating them to anyone else — and said, 'No of course not. I would not expect it. I am well satisfied studying your book. What a terrible occurrence. Is there anything I can do?'

He gave a bitter laugh. 'I suppose returning to last week and dissuading me from coming into Cambridgeshire at all is out of the question? I am presently sincerely regretting the haven of peace and tranquillity comprising my sister-in-law's descent on the town house.'

She smiled. 'It will pass.' A thought darted into her head. Overcoming her distaste at deceiving Edward, she added, 'I am afraid your servants will be much discomposed by this news. Shall I leave Woods with you for the present to maintain order in the household?'

He gazed at her as if she had said something miraculous. 'Beyond rubies,' he said. 'Your worth is most definitely beyond rubies. I accept with thanks.'

The guilt was unbearable. Lilith rose, only just not fleeing from the gratitude in his eyes. 'I shall tell him. I will not be many minutes. I will also ask Peter to bring you some refreshment. You look in pressing need of it.'

'Neatly done,' murmured Hester as they ascended the staircase to the secretary's room, where Woods was still nominally helping Ferris with the patient.

'I dislike misleading him,' said Lilith shortly. 'Nor do I like leaving him and

Ricky in such disarray, but Kerr must be sequestered in some fashion and Woods is the best person to arrange that. I have to talk to Mr Dacre. We must get word to my brother to have Kerr investigated.'

Because she refused, she *refused*, to think Edward had anything to do with his secretary's quest to *find Mrs Eastwick*.

★   ★   ★

Nicholas Dacre swore, softly and vehemently. 'Tell me again,' he said. His hand remained clasped around Catherine's.

'Just that,' replied Lilith. She had not stopped to change her shoes or take off her bonnet before seeking him out in Catherine's sitting room. 'Nothing else. '*Must find Mrs Eastwick. Not at church. Must send word.*' That was all Kerr said. He was threshing about and mostly incoherent.'

'No one heard him?'

'Only Woods, Hester and me. It is why I have just sent Woods back there with his belongings, though I would have offered to loan him to Edward in any case with the house in such turmoil. We may see Edward and Ricky here this evening, Catherine. The cook is sitting in the kitchen wailing and beating her breast. Why she should be more upset with Atkins dead than when she thought he had absconded without her I cannot imagine, but so it is. I doubt any food worth eating will be prepared in Ditton Place today.'

'You like Makepeace?' Nicholas's gaze was direct.

Lilith straightened her back. 'I believe him to be a good man, yes.'

'Yet you said nothing to him regarding his secretary?'

Lilith took a moment before answering. There was a small part of her chest that tore every time she thought about this. 'How could I?' she said at last. 'I would trust him with *my* life. I cannot make that decision for Catherine. I am

. . . not happy . . . about the situation.'

Catherine moved across to Lilith, taking her hands in both her own. 'Thank you,' she said. 'It is never easy being forced to question one's trust. I thought when I escaped to Newmarket it would be an end to the fear. I was wrong. Flint's web, his creeping tendrils, will go on ruining people and poisoning lives until he is unmasked and dealt with. Nicholas and Benedict and their friends may never know how many people Flint was blackmailing. As it is, suspicion seeps into everything. I am so sorry.'

Lilith was shaken by the other woman's sincerity. Shaken and ashamed. She was being selfish. 'Then we must search Flint out,' she said resolutely. 'Will you ask Benedict to investigate Donald Kerr, Nicholas? For my part, I can very easily find out from Edward how long he has employed him and what he knows of his history. That would be normal, polite interest — nothing to raise any suspicions.'

'I'll write to your brother now and get the letter off by tonight's mail.' He gave his rare smile. 'Thank you.'

He didn't say what for, and Lilith didn't ask him. She wasn't sure she was ready to hear the answer.

In her own room, soothed by slippers, a warm fire, hot washing water and a tray of Catherine's excellent tea and seed cake, Lilith set herself to think. *It is never easy being forced to question one's trust.* All Lilith's instincts were to trust Edward Makepeace. That was why she was hurting so much.

Very well. She would apply logic. She had known him such a short time. Why *should* she trust him? She pulled her sketchbook towards her and began to make notes. Disregarding his glorious, many-shaded fair hair, good looks and broad frame as frivolous reasons, what else was there?

He treated her as a person. He was solicitous of his brother. He had the sort of intelligence that was always willing to learn. He was not complacent. He never doubted her intelligence. He was exasperated when things went wrong, but it didn't occur to him to shirk putting them right. He was generous with praise. He let her speak for herself. He listened to what she had to say. He helped her over rough ground. He made her laugh.

At this point, Lilith decided her list might be a little less than impartial. 'What am I to do?' she said with a sigh.

Hester glanced across from where she was laying out an evening gown. 'Talk to him, Miss Lilith. Oh, not about *that*, though I can't see how you'll avoid it. Talk about his family, books, travels. You can't decide until you know him, can you?'

Decide what? But Hester was still speaking. 'The other thing you can do,' she said, 'is to find him a housekeeper. And a different cook. That Mrs Bell is a disgrace.'

Lilith laughed. 'Shall I go upstairs and intrude on Mrs Smith then? It

191

seems a shame as the child is quiet for once.' Then she chuckled some more to see Hester settling herself in the corner with some mending. 'Hester, is that Ricky's shirt?'

Hester sniffed. 'I can't abide idle hands, Miss Lilith, and he doesn't appear to have anyone else to do it bar Mr Ferris, who has enough to do without mending ripped seams.'

Lightened beyond measure by Hester's clear approval of both Edward and his brother, Lilith tore her list up. Instead she sketched Ricky, striding tall and eager along the dyke, declaiming to the wind.

11

'I have induced Mrs Bell to commence stewing mutton for the men's meal,' said Woods deferentially as he placed a tankard by Ned's elbow, 'but you and Mr Richard and Mr Thornley may prefer to dine out.'

Which was a circumspect way of saying the results were likely to be inedible. 'Ever considered becoming a butler, Woods?' asked Ned.

'I am in Lord Fitzgilbert's service, sir.'

'Yes, of course you are. Pity.' Ned unenthusiastically reviewed his options. He couldn't eat at the Three Blackbirds in the village, not with Atkins laid out in the back room there, waiting for the inquest tomorrow. He supposed he could join Thornley in whichever of the Newmarket hotels he had selected for tonight's dalliance, or . . . 'In your opinion,' he said, striving for a note of off-hand enquiry, 'would it look in any way particular should I call at Furze House again this evening?'

'Not if you were to take Mr Richard with you, sir. I'd say it would be perfectly understandable.'

'You're a sensible man, Woods. I can now collate this afternoon's results with far more heart.'

Ferris was equally approving. Ned assumed this was because he and Ricky would *both* have to be smartly dressed for once, but Ferris had another motive.

'If you could perhaps call on the doctor on your way, sir? I don't like the look of Mr Kerr.'

Ned frowned. 'Is he still disturbed?'

'The reverse. I might almost describe him as comatose.'

Ferris was right. Kerr's breathing was laboured. The pupils of his eyes, when the valet wordlessly lifted an eyelid, were pinpricks. Ned looked at them with misgivings. 'I'll tell the doctor,' he said, adding, 'The man might as well move in, he has been here so often today.'

He and Ricky arrived at Furze House to the same unruffled reception as the previous evening. 'You will be thinking I am taking up residence,' he said to Nicholas Dacre who once more materialised from the stables and accompanied them to the saloon.

Lilith looked up with a smile and closed her sketchbook as they entered. Ned found himself smiling back. Was it really less than a week ago that he'd viewed her possible descent on Ditton Place with horror?

'Not at all,' replied Dacre. 'You are very welcome. I frequently find myself outnumbered. How goes it at Ditton Place? Lilith told us the latest news. You must have been very much shocked.'

'Lilith . . . ' repeated Ricky, charmed. 'I like it. Have you had many poems written about your name?'

'Many,' said Lilith with feeling. 'Is your secretary any better, Edward? Has he said how he came to fall?'

'He hasn't said anything,' replied Ned. 'He remains deeply asleep. Ferris thinks it is unnatural and so do I. The doctor is going to call early tomorrow.'

'I hope it is nothing too alarming. You will not wish to be without his help for any great length of time. Has he been in your employ long?'

'Three years. Originally we thought Ricky might share some of the estate tasks with me, but his studies took too much of a toll on him, so I made the decision to engage a professional.'

'What Ned means is that the whole business bewildered me,' said Ricky cheerfully. 'All those columns of figures in the ledger on the one hand, and the letters with wool returns and requests for repairs to hedges and roads on the other . . . I couldn't see how anything related to anything else at all.'

Ned winced, remembering. 'It was certainly interesting, disentangling your attempts. At any event, Donald Kerr came with excellent references and proved exactly what I wanted.' *And if he wasn't congenial, at least he was efficient. You couldn't have everything.*

'I would have no idea how to engage a secretary,' mused Lilith. 'I believe Benedict's man was recommended to him by a friend. Does one go to a registry office as one does for a maid or a footman?'

'That's certainly what I did,' replied Ned, 'after asking around to no avail first. Talking of which, I had best call into the Newmarket bureau tomorrow morning. Kerr will not be up to sorting out extra staff for some time.' He paused. 'Might I direct my carriage here to wait for me and then convey you to Ditton Place when my business is finished? It would save your own coachman from turning out. None of us will be there during the afternoon because we are required at the inquest, but you are welcome to read up more of the subject in the library.'

'That sounds very agreeable,' replied Lilith tranquilly. 'Thank you.'

'It will find favour with Fred Grimes

too,' remarked Catherine, entering the room. 'It is Molly's laundry round tomorrow and they are building up a regular clientele.'

Ned immediately got to his feet and introduced Ricky, trying very hard not to laugh at the smitten look on his brother's face. 'I don't think you will need to worry overmuch about odes to your name,' he murmured to Lilith. 'If Ricky is not right now seeking a rhyme for *Catherine* I don't know him nearly as well as I thought I did.'

Lilith chuckled. 'She is very beautiful, isn't she? I have been ruining page after page of my sketchbook trying to draw her and not doing her justice in the least.'

'I am sure that is not true. May I see?'

'No, or you will spend all evening knowing I am a failure which is very lowering to the spirits. However, I did a sketch of your brother that I am vainly pleased with. I will show you after we have eaten, and then you will go home thinking I am remarkably clever and will have no qualms about my borrowing any books I choose from your library.'

Just for a moment, her laughing grey-green eyes had a constricting effect on Ned's breathing. Whatever was happening to him? 'My shelves are at your disposal,' he said, spreading his hands. 'I had best rescue your friend from Ricky or we shall never be invited again.'

And that was a stupid thing to say, for they hadn't been invited this time. They had simply turned up. What in the world was wrong with him tonight?

★　★　★

'Another wonderful meal, Catherine,' said Lilith as Ned helped her to cutlets in a butter sauce. 'Far better than your scholars will be eating, Edward. I do feel rather guilty about poor Woods. Perhaps after the inquest tomorrow your cook will put aside her grief and pull herself together.'

'I sincerely hope so. Mrs Bell's menus are rarely inspired, but she has never been this bad before. If I was feeling charitable, I might ascribe it to her additional domestic duties, though I see little sign of them either. I begin to wonder if my housekeeper did more than I realised.'

'Almost certainly,' agreed Catherine across the table. 'I had no idea how much work was involved in running a house, and how time-consuming it was, until I . . . until I set up my own establishment.'

Ned politely affected not to notice the warning flicker Nicholas Dacre sent her. There was evidently some story there, but it was none of his business. He lifted his glass. 'To all invisible staff. I must remember to send especial thanks to the kitchen when I return to London for my dinner for potential investors in the Greek project. This has been an eye-opening visit in more ways than one.'

'When is your dinner?' asked Dacre.

'Next week. Would you like to come?'

The other man laughed. 'It would be under false pretences if I did. The polite world knows I have not a feather to fly with of my own. This is why I am trying to build up my matched-pair stables here, so I have a little independence from my grandfather.'

'I meant as a friend and supporter, not as an investor.'

'Oh, that's a different matter. I'll come to your dinner if you'll brace me next month at my grandfather's birthday ball. I am going to have to do the pretty to so many guests I am likely to run half of them through if I do not have friends to tease me into a better humour at regular intervals.'

'It seems a fair exchange.'

'Benedict and I will be there as well, Nicholas,' Lilith said. She gave a tiny frown as if calculating dates. 'Yes, I will be back in Bedford Square by then.'

'I will miss you,' said Catherine. 'I like having the house occupied.'

'It won't be for long,' said Lilith with a smile. 'I daresay Ver . . . very many other ladies will descend on you for a restorative spell in the country.'

'Do they expect to find out tomorrow why your butler absconded?' asked Dacre, changing the subject abruptly.

'We know why,' replied Ricky. 'Because we'd discovered he was robbing Ned. He'd dismissed the staff and was taking their wages for himself.'

'How much had he stolen? Was he making off with anything else of value?'

Ned frowned. 'No, I suppose he must have spent the money. I checked the bags, but there were only clothes and shaving gear in them, hastily packed.' He tailed off, his throat suddenly arid.

'And?' prodded Dacre.

Ned met his eyes. 'Atkins's valises were dry,' he said slowly. 'I have only just realised. Both bags and contents, and the shirt that had spilled out of one of them. Everything was dry.'

It wasn't just Dacre who was alert to the change in his voice now. Lilith dropped her cutlery with a clatter and put her hands to her mouth, staring at him in horror.

'And no money in either of them,' said Ricky. 'I went through them with Ned.'

'But Edward, they couldn't have been,' said Lilith, speaking directly to him as if there was no one else in the room. 'Atkins was wet though. You said so.'

Ned felt as though the pit of his stomach had dropped away. Someone had known where Atkins was. Someone had gone back to the ditch after the rain had stopped and thrown his bags after him. 'How?' he whispered, still looking at Lilith. 'Who?'

The horrified silence was broken by Catherine. 'Eat,' she said, leaning across and tapping Ned's plate. 'Money is not so abundant in this house that we can afford waste. Problems are more easily solved on a full stomach than on an empty one.'

Everyone muttered a hasty apology and continued with their meal, though as far as Ned was concerned, it might just as well have been one of Mrs Bell's efforts for all he tasted it.

'When did it stop raining?' said Lilith with practical good sense. 'It was wet when I retired last night. I listened to raindrops being flung against the window for some time before I fell asleep. You certainly grow fierce winds in this part of the country.'

'I woke at seven, I think,' said Ned. 'The rain had stopped by then.'

'It was dry by five o'clock,' put in Ricky. 'Something woke me — I don't know what — and I got out of bed and stood looking at the gardens. Such a fey scene, Ned, it was as still as a folk tale. The moonlight glittered on the wet grass. If I had seen naiads and dryads I should not have been in the least surprised.'

'And how long did you freeze there, waiting for them? Sometimes I despair

of you, Ricky. You know how susceptible . . . '

'Peace,' said his brother fondly.
'Ferris had built up the fire overnight
and I wrapped myself in the counter-
pane. Anyway, I saw Peter come out of
the kitchen wing and cough in the night
air, so I went back to bed. I didn't want
anybody spoiling my nice scene.'

Five o'clock, thought Ned guiltily.
And the young footman had still been
on duty in the hall at midnight. How
early did his servants get up?

Across the table from him, Lilith said
reluctantly, 'Peter said his older sister
was a maid at Ditton Place before
Atkins became too familiar and she
left.'

'No,' said Ned forcefully. 'I don't
believe it. Not about Atkins,' he added,
'I believe *that*, but I don't believe Peter
Swann would have . . . ' He paused.
'What would he have had to do? Follow
Atkins, give him a push at the vital
moment, bring the valises back here to
ransack and then dispose of them a day

later to cover his tracks? I can't see it.'

Was that another flicker of a glance between Dacre and Catherine? Dacre cleared his throat and looked at Ned straightly. 'Somebody did. The question is, do you want the coroner to arrest your footman on no evidence bar a historic grudge?'

'No, I damn well don't. If I'd had a sister in the same situation, Atkins wouldn't have stayed alive long enough to continue working for me. But how can we stop him? The jury will all be local. They'll know the history. And they all hate me because of Atkins firing most of the staff.'

'They'll hate Atkins worse,' said Dacre shrewdly. 'If you don't mention the circumstance of his valises being dry, I'd wager my best team they won't ask.'

'Suppress evidence? I can't do that.'

Dacre made an impatient gesture. 'Not *volunteering* evidence isn't the same as suppressing it. Think man, an accidental verdict leaves you with a free hand to find out the facts for yourself. Time enough then to alert the authorities, if that's what you decide to do.'

Ned gazed at him, troubled. The thought of his gawky, fresh-faced young footman being incarcerated in the county gaol while he waited for the quarterly assizes was appalling. He nodded. 'Is that all right with you, Ricky? We don't mention the condition of the valises unless we are asked?' He'd have to warn Chilcott too. The groom had helped him lift the bags out of the ditch.

'Oh yes,' said Ricky cheerfully. 'I liked Peter's sister. She used to make up my fire when we were here before. I asked Peter where she was and he says she's got a position at the rectory now.'

'Which she'd lose if this came to light,' said Ned heavily. 'A clerical household can't be seen to be employing servants with dubious reputations. You're right, Dacre. We say nothing.' *And perhaps some time you will tell me the real reason why.*

12

The next morning, the doctor pronounced Kerr's breathing to be a little
easier, but admitted himself puzzled by
the heavy sleep. 'He looks to be heavily
drugged, yet there is hardly any gone
from the bottle. It may be he has an
idiosyncrasy for laudanum. Has he ever
mentioned as much?'

'No,' replied Ned, 'but I disremem-
ber him ever being ill before. He seems
impervious to extreme weather and
keeps going far longer than we do.
Indeed, Kerr is usually the one who
physics the rest of us. He has the knack
of knowing what will help.'

The doctor allowed Woods to help
him into his greatcoat, then took his hat
and gloves. 'I cannot account for it
apart from an idiosyncrasy. If that is the
case, you must simply wait until it has
taken its course. His head seems only

grazed. His ankle is severely swollen. That will come down with cold bandages and rest. Good day. I daresay I will see you this afternoon at the inquest.'

'Indeed. Until this afternoon, then. My thanks for coming out again.'

'I'll add it to my account,' said the doctor drily.

Ned chuckled and put on his own hat and gloves. He was on the point of leaving when he exclaimed aloud in consternation. 'It's all very well going to the registry office for more servants, but I don't know who I need.'

Woods deferentially passed him a sheet of paper. 'I took the liberty of writing it down for you sir.' He nodded to Peter. 'Hand your master into the carriage like we practised.'

'Righto, Mr Woods,' said Peter cheerfully.

Ned folded the list, biting his lips together in an effort not to smile.

It wasn't very long before he was presenting himself at Furze House.

'Good morning,' Lilith greeted him. 'I am quite ready. Have you discharged all your business?'

He adopted a suitably grave expression. 'Yes indeed, but with a heavy heart.'

Lilith's eyes twinkled. 'And why is that?'

'Because it occurred to me even as I put in the request that as soon as I have competent servants again, I shall have to relinquish Woods.'

'Into every life a little rain must fall. That was told to me by a particularly lachrymose governess. Do you remember her, Hester? Miss Potts.'

Behind them, Lilith's maid sniffed portentously. 'She wasn't so tearful out of the house. You wouldn't hardly recognise her on her half-day off.'

'Really? Is that why she left so suddenly? I thought Mama must have become exasperated with her habit of bursting into tears whenever she looked at the garden in the square. I asked her about it once and she told me she missed the country.'

'She missed country ways, more like,' muttered Hester, and Ned tried not to splutter with amusement. 'We all knew downstairs who it was borrowed the key to the garden four nights out of seven. Small wonder she had to be packed off back to her vicarage. She wrote your ma she'd married the squire's son, the same one she was forever disparaging when she was here. Didn't surprise me. He sounded a right slow-top, and she couldn't afford to let the grass grow under her feet, not for a moment.'

Ned chuckled. Lilith took a little longer to follow Hester's drift, then looked at her maid, round-eyed as they settled themselves in the carriage. 'Good heavens. I didn't have the slightest inkling. Not that I know precisely what you are talking about, you understand. Well, that shows you can never take anyone at face value, doesn't it?'

At Ditton Place, Ned conducted the

ladies to the library and explained to Lilith the reasons behind the reading he had selected for her today. 'But if it proves too dry for you, do choose anything else from the shelves,' he said. Then he went upstairs for Ferris to turn him into the polished semblance of a responsible local landowner ready for the inquest. 'I'm putting that coat back on again when I return,' he warned his valet. 'Don't go losing it or sending it to be laundered.'

'No sir, though Mrs Turner's work has been exemplary.'

'Mrs Turner?' Ned looked at Ferris, mystified.

'Mrs Turner's laundry at the rear of Furze House. Mr Woods recommended it, so I have been sending her the linen with Chilcott, there not being sufficient servants here to see to it. Also Mr Kerr's sheets, which were in sad need of . . .'

'Yes, yes, yes. I don't need the details,' said Ned hastily. 'Well done, Ferris. Thank you.'

Was he particularly blind or self-centred? he wondered. He was reminded of Catherine's observation that she had no idea what went into the running of a house until she set up her own establishment. Just how much else went on underneath the outer skin of Ditton Place that he was unaware of?

★   ★   ★

Lilith read studiously until the gentlemen had departed for the inquest. Then she closed her book — with some regret, because it was an interesting topic — and said, 'Hester, how remiss of us. We have not enquired about poor Mr Kerr. We should do so without delay. I daresay Ferris will be glad to have someone to sit with his patient for a little while, and I can read just as easily up there as I can here.'

Much as she abhorred her actions, she had to find out if there was anything amongst Kerr's belongings

213

relating to Flint. Deceiving Edward might not be the same level of danger that Verity and Catherine had encountered recently, but it was quite the most unpleasant thing Lilith had ever had to do. She needed to straighten her spine and get on with it before distaste for her task overcame her.

Edward's valet was pleased to see them. 'Not that I think he'll give you any trouble, for he's still sleeping and I've only been popping in and out myself, but I'd like to get my gentlemen's rooms tidied before they return.' He hesitated on the threshold. 'It might be as well to call Mr Woods up in case he suddenly wakes out of his mind. Mr Richard did that one time and it took two of us to stop him rushing out of doors in his night-clothes.' He glanced again at the man in the bed. 'You wouldn't think it, but Mr Kerr is a deal stronger than he seems. He told me once it was growing up in Scotland as did it, but I don't see how that can be.'

As it suited Lilith very well to have Woods on watch outside the door, she agreed to the suggestion immediately. 'Now, Hester, we may not have long, so where should we look for information linking Kerr to Flint?' The prying itself was far less repugnant to her than the fact of doing it without Edward's knowledge.

Hester assessed the room. 'I'll check the pockets of his clothes. You see if there's anything in the desk.'

Lilith nodded and moved swiftly into the study. It was a ruthlessly tidy room furnished in the style of an earlier age with, Lilith saw with a sinking heart, many boxes and drawers where papers could be stacked. 'This is going to take forever,' she said in despair.

She started with the boxes on the desk, but a quick riffle through the top two showed they only held papers relating to the farms. The third seemed to be correspondence with the Foreign Office regarding Edward's proposed summer investigations in Greece.

She next tried the desk, but was frustrated to find every drawer locked. 'Keys, Hester,' she said, darting back through the connecting door. 'Have you found any?'

'On the nightstand next to his pocketbook. I took a peek, but it's in that cramped a hand . . . '

'I'll look if we have time. I'll check the drawers first.'

She ran back and tried the smaller keys in turn, conscious that Ferris might return at any moment. The relief as a key turned at last was short-lived. The top left-hand drawer merely held a bundle of letters from his mother. Lilith flicked through them, turning them to skim the crossed lines, feeling more uncomfortable than ever at the intrusion, but they were just thanks for gifts, snippets of local gossip, a mention that his stepfather's new apprentice was settling in nicely and laments about never seeing him apart from Hogmanay. Lilith relocked the drawer and tried the next one down. She had completed the left-hand side of the kneehole desk and was about to move across to the right when she heard Woods greeting Ferris in the passage.

'Nothing,' she said, whisking back into the bedroom and speedily returning the keys to the nightstand. 'Ledgers, bank books, payments and receipts in abundance, and bills from his tailor and bootmaker. We may get a chance to look at the rest another time.'

Ferris's entrance coincided with a groan from the bed and some murmuring.

'Is he waking?' said Lilith, looking up from her book brightly. 'Will he be able to tell us what happened?'

'He hasn't done so far,' replied Edward's valet. 'Mouthful of lemon barley, a few drops of laudanum and he's back to sleep. I'll see to him now, miss. I saw from the window the gentlemen were coming up the drive. Mr Woods has gone down to organise refreshment.'

Lilith obediently carried her unread

book back to the library. At least she now had Kerr's Scottish address and his stepfather's name for Benedict's agents to follow up.

★　★　★

The function room of the Three Blackbirds was a good size for a village inn, but was uncomfortably full of people. The party from Ditton Place sat in the first two rows, aware of an unexpectedly hostile scrutiny from the rest of the room.

'Why do they dislike us?' whispered Ricky, shifting awkwardly on the hard bench.

'I don't know,' murmured Ned. His brother, always sensitive to atmosphere, was correct. Chilcott had said the inn as a whole had seemed more unfriendly than during their previous visits, but the feeling right now had overtones of actual hatred.

The coroner was not minded to dally. The formalities were swiftly dealt with, the doctor gave it as his opinion that a fall of fifteen feet followed by a cold night had been the cause of death, and then the questions began. Ned didn't mention the condition of Atkins's valises, simply stated that the last time he had seen the butler was the evening before his disappearance, when they'd had strong words on the subject of the ill-preparedness of the house, the unacceptable lack of staff, the missing dozen bottles of wine and Atkins's general philandering. 'It has since transpired that he dismissed the staff on his own initiative and was keeping their wages for himself. If I'd known that, I would have let him go on the spot.'

There was a murmur in the room. The jury looked significantly at one another.

Ricky agreed that was what had taken place and said his brother's secretary had also been present, but had tripped on a fallen tree yesterday morning and was now lying in bed with an injured leg and a shaken head so he couldn't attend today.

This was confirmed by the doctor. The coroner asked the servants about Atkins's mood.

'Furious fit to burst, he was,' said Peter. 'He's not an easy man, but he was worse than I've ever seen him. Swearing something terrible about people what thought they were so high and mighty. And Mrs Bell weeping and wailing and him shouting at her to hold her whist and what had she got to complain about? I slid out of the kitchen sharpish. Didn't surprise me he'd loped off come the morning.'

The maids nodded feverish agreement. Everyone had finished their tasks as soon as possible and kept out of his way. There had been no sign of him next day. Sleeping it off, had been the consensus. When Peter had eventually tapped at his door and gone in, the room was empty.

It didn't take long for the jury to come to their conclusion. The foreman, whom Ned recognised as the village blacksmith, stood up and cleared his throat. 'What we think is that Mr Atkins brought it upon himself.'

The coroner looked at him wearily. 'Would you care to explain that?'

There was nothing the foreman would like more. 'He brought it on himself, a'cos if he hadn't turned off George Sixsmith the head gardener and Will Thorpe who used to keep that path down to the lane clear, he wouldn't have missed his way when he was scarpering and he wouldn't have fallen down the ditch and met his grisly end.'

The coroner, evidently well used to village jurors, sighed. 'I'll record it as accidental death.'

'More like God's judgement,' objected the blacksmith.

'Maybe so,' said the coroner, 'but Mr Atkins didn't miss his way on purpose, did he? So it must have been accidental.'

There was a discontented grumble from the jury. 'Accident what he brought on himself,' amended the blacksmith. 'We'd also like it to go on record that anyone laying off God-fearing folk is asking for trouble, whether it's shifty, no-good butlers or people who should know better.' This last was said with a glassy stare at the Ditton Place bench. Ned wondered which of his family had used to be employed in the house.

'Yes, yes, the clerk will write it all down,' said the coroner testily. 'I declare the proceedings closed. Good day, gentlemen.'

Ned stood, ignoring the wave of righteousness sweeping the room and strode over to the rector. He collected the landlord with his eye too. 'Reverend, the landlord is no doubt wanting his room back as soon as possible. I will cover the cost of the burial. Mr Atkins was nominally in my employ, even though he wouldn't have been a day later. After what we have heard, I doubt there will be many mourners, but the thing should be done decently. Will you see to it and send the account to Ditton Place?'

The rector inclined his head. 'Certainly, Mr Makepeace. Even a rogue should be allowed a chance in the hereafter.'

Ned didn't quite trust himself to reply to that. He turned to the landlord. 'You have the ear of the village. If Atkins turned off any who are still without work, I'll be glad to take them back. I will be available at Ditton Place tomorrow morning to sign on anyone who wishes to return.'

He got a long stare. 'All of them, would that be, sir?'

Ned frowned. What was the man getting at? 'Certainly. The dismissals were made without my knowledge or agreement.'

The landlord nodded, unsmiling. 'I'll put the word around.'

Ricky was waiting for him by the door. They followed the others back to Ditton Place, walking fast to shake off the oppressive atmosphere of the inn.

'Can I help you tomorrow?' asked Ricky. 'I can take names and write down what folk used to do. I don't want you facing that ... that dislike by yourself.'

Ned looked sideways, touched. 'Thank you. I'd like that. I wish I knew the reason for the unpleasantness.'

'They might tell us once they have their positions back. I don't like being hated, Ned.'

He was looking unhappy. Ned felt a trickle of worry. Being in low spirits was what had previously had Ricky reaching for the laudanum. 'It's too much to hope that there are any assistant cooks amongst them, don't you think?' he said. 'I was going to suggest we went to the inn to eat tonight, but after today's proceedings I can face that even less than I can face one of Mrs Bell's dinners. Do you suppose if we look plaintive, Lilith will invite us to Furze House again?'

His brother brightened immediately.

'Oh yes, rather. Won't the others think we are abandoning them?'

'They are receiving free board and lodging. I made no promises as to quality.'

13

Lilith saw at once that though the inquest had produced the desired result, there was something else bothering Edward. With a practised smile, she disengaged herself from Mr Thornley's ready flow of conversation, saying he would no doubt wish to get his men outside to make up for the loss of time. Moving to Edward, she asked whether the sad business was now over.

'Yes,' he said. 'I've told the rector to send the account for the burial to me. I daresay Kerr will scold me for the expense, but I do not think I could have done ought else.'

Lilith nodded. 'I agree. There are times when conventions may be flouted, but a death touches everyone in a close community such as a village, whether the departed was liked or not. You did exactly right and if you have to go without a remove at dinner, or put one less log on the fire this evening, so be it. It serves no purpose to be parsimonious.'

'Thank you. I thought you would understand.'

He was still unhappy though. Lilith set herself to lighten his mood. 'You begin to know me, then? How discouraging.'

'Only in matters of sense and decorum,' Edward assured her. 'In all other matters you are as much of a surprise as ever.'

She laughed. 'Now you are talking nearly as much nonsense as Mr Thornley. But I *am* glad you are doing the right thing.'

'You will not be pleased though, that I must put off your teaching for another day. I have said I will be at home tomorrow for any of our former servants to reapply for their positions.'

'How could I be displeased at that? I shall steal an armload of your folios and devour them greedily in one of the alcoves. Unless you feel you will need help?'

'Ricky has offered to assist. The only difficulty is not knowing the previous list of staff and how much they were being paid. It is to both our shame that we do not recall the names already. Crow at me if you must, but I do now realise I leave too much to Kerr. Do you suppose there would be a tally of the servants in the butler's pantry or the housekeeper's room?'

Lilith, with what she couldn't help feeling was a touch of greatness, seized the moment. 'Your secretary will have the details. I noticed when Hester and I went to spell Ferris that there were a number of boxes on his desk. Why not have a look through those?'

'Admirable idea. Have you been acting as nurse? That is not why you are here.'

Deceiving him was bad. Being praised undeservedly was awful. 'Like you, I find I can only ignore my sense of duty so far. We sat there while your valet was about his normal tasks, and I took Sir Richard Colt Hoare's *Recollections Abroad* with me to study. I have never been to Sicily. It sounds most interesting, but the method of travel, carrying everything with him, seems very time-consuming and arduous in nature.'

'It can be so indeed, which is why it cost us so much for the porters and the litters in Egypt. Will you excuse me? I must change into my comfortable clothes before Ferris puts them out for the poorhouse. We were also going to ask, Ricky and I, whether we might dine at Furze House tonight?'

'You would be very welcome. By the by, your post was delivered while you were at the inquest. Much of it seems to have been sent on from London. Woods did not know what your custom was, so he has put it on a pile on the side table there.'

Edward glanced unenthusiastically at the weighty bundle of letters. He looked towards his brother, but Ricky had already withdrawn into his muse, reading over scattered pages of stanzas and making corrections to them.

Lilith chuckled. 'I have never seen such a picture of reluctance. Will you allow me to help? I can very easily look through the ledgers for your staff list whilst you deal with the correspondence.'

'You are not here to . . . '

She laid a hand on his. It was warm under her palm, strong and square, accustomed to working physically as well as writing learned papers. 'We will get to antiquarian affairs a lot faster by despatching business matters first.'

Edward sighed. 'Your strength of will is extraordinary. Miss Fitzgilbert, if you would be so very kind, could I trouble you to open the letters and sort them into personal, business and antiquarian matters while I change my clothes? I shall not keep you above a quarter of an hour.'

It was not quite what Lilith had been hoping for, but with any luck once she had sorted the letters, he would regard her as an assistant and she could progress to searching through the remaining locked drawers in Kerr's desk.

There was one letter from his sister-in-law, several very obviously antiquarian queries, and then a letter with Lord Hazelmere's seal on the reverse.

Lord Hazelmere presents his compliments and is pleased to accept your invitation to a dinner and presentation on Grecian Antiquities at Ditton Place, Cambridgeshire.

Lilith sat up straight, her heart thudding in dismay. Ditton Place? Lord Hazelmere thought the dinner was at Ditton Place? She swallowed down her apprehension and hastily broke the seal of the next letter.

By the time Edward reappeared she had several piles of letters. By far the largest followed the pattern of Lord Hazelmere's.

'Edward,' she said. 'When is your

dinner for potential investors being held?'

'Next week. The twenty-sixth. You were there when I told Nicholas Dacre.' He glanced at the letters and saw the tell-tale purple of his sister-in-law's missive. Apprehension crossed his face. 'Don't tell me Leonora has arranged something for then? I asked Kerr specifically to let her and Henry know when it was.'

'Your sister-in-law doesn't mention it at all.'

'Oh, good.'

'Largely, I imagine, because it is not taking place in the town house. It is being held here.'

'Here?' Edward stared at her in horror. 'With Mrs Bell presiding over the kitchen? It cannot be. I cannot hold it here. You must be mistaken.'

Lilith handed him the sheaf of acceptances. 'There are some dozen titled and influential gentlemen who are equally mistaken, then. Did you write to them yourself?'

'No, Kerr sent out all the invitations.' Edward looked through the replies, the colour draining from his face. He sat heavily in the chair next to her. 'The dinner was to be arranged with the chef at the town house. I know it was. How can Kerr have got it wrong?'

'He must have misunderstood you.'

'No one can misunderstand how I feel about Mrs Bell's cooking.'

'Well then, might he have arranged for a local chef to come in?'

Edward grasped at this slender straw. 'That is possible, yes. I need to look at his correspondence without delay.'

As this accorded exactly with Lilith's wishes, she didn't point out that the easiest way to find out what was planned was to ask Mrs Bell herself. 'May I assist?' she said instead. 'It will be faster with two of us.'

He stood up, purpose in every line of him. 'Thank you. I would be very grateful.'

Kerr's rooms were exactly as Lilith and Hester had left them earlier. 'Any

233

change?' Edward asked Ferris.

The valet shrugged. 'His breathing worsened for a bit and he's been mumbling. Nothing to the purpose.'

Edward directed a look of frustration at the bed. 'I still cannot believe he has got it so wrong. There must be an explanation in the correspondence.'

'There are no letters on the desk,' said Lilith. 'Do you have his keys?' She stood by the right-hand side of the desk, making it natural that she would start there while he took the other. The first drawer held a locked wooden box. Lilith found the key and opened it quickly, before Edward could wonder why she might expect to find dinner information amongst personal possessions. Sadly, the box simply contained a small amount of money, two signet rings, a sprig of heather and a loose pebble. The second drawer produced gold as far as the dinner was concerned, but nothing to advance her own personal search. Lilith cast a surreptitious glance sideways. Would Edward notice if she opened the bottom drawer as well? She located the correct key.

He put back the bundle of letters. 'All cross-written. I can make nothing of them. But I suppose Kerr would hardly be writing to his mother about my Greek presentation.'

'It seems unlikely,' agreed Lilith. She passed across the correspondence she had found. 'These are all replies about your dinner. There is no doubt it is intended to be held here. There is nothing regarding who is to order it or cook it. You had best find out from Mrs Bell what the arrangements are to be.'

In the corner of the room, Hester gave an eloquent sniff. Ferris exchanged a glance with her and pursed his lips. 'Mrs Bell has not mentioned it, sir,' he said. 'The amount she's been complaining ever since we arrived, I would have expected her to be listing it as another grievance if it was her who was to do it.'

Edward grimaced. 'You see my quandary?' he said to Lilith. 'If I ask, she will instantly assume responsibility for the whole, which would be a disaster of the first water. I would rather send out cards to cancel the whole affair and forego the summer expedition entirely. I was hoping to find some indication of Kerr's arrangements before broaching the matter, but there is nothing for it, I shall ask. I must remind myself not to compensate for my dislike of her by being over-fair and giving in.' His eyes met Lilith's. 'Unless . . . no, I cannot ask it of you.'

Lilith's sense of propriety was rocked. 'Edward! I have no authority in this house. I cannot speak to your cook. It would be strange in the extreme.'

'No. And you are here to study, not act as a temporary chatelaine. My apologies. It was cowardly of me to even think it.'

Lilith opened the last drawer without being aware of her action. Ledgers. Nothing personal at all. Beside her, she could feel Edward's wretchedness. She couldn't bear it. 'However,' she said slowly, 'I *am* accustomed to dealing with housekeepers, butlers and the most temperamental of chefs — and I suppose as your newest scholar I may claim to have an interest in the future of your expedition. Let me see. You are interviewing your former servants tomorrow. I could say to Mrs Bell that with these interviews in mind, you had asked me to find out how she was fixed in the kitchen, whether she had enough help, that sort of thing. From that, I can pass to other matters. If I use the housekeeper's room to interview her, it will invest me with authority by association.'

His expression of hope was ridiculously endearing and did very odd things to her chest. 'Can you ask without promising her anything?'

Lilith gave him a disbelieving look. 'Edward, I have been supervising my father's house since I was seventeen. Trust me, I can manage a country cook.'

★   ★   ★

'Good afternoon, Mrs Bell. I expect you are wondering why I asked to see you. Mr Makepeace is finding out about the state of the household with the intention of increasing the complement of servants, but he has no experience of the domestic side of things. In the absence of a housekeeper, he wondered if I could discuss matters with you. For example, how are you situated as regards kitchen maids for your day-to-day needs?'

Mrs Bell, an unlovely woman who had evidently been fortifying herself after the ordeal of the inquest, swayed gently and edged towards the stability of the housekeeper's table where Lilith was sitting. 'Could always use another,' she said guardedly.

Lilith made a note. 'And if Mr Makepeace were to entertain? Do you have enough kitchen staff to ensure the event runs smoothly?'

'Him? He don't entertain.'

'But suppose he did?'

'I weren't engaged for no fancy

238

dinners, but it makes no odds because he's too tight-fisted to give them. Wouldn't have put everyone on half-wages if he wasn't.'

Lilith made another calm note. 'Oh, did he do so? I had not realised. When was this?'

'Soon as he went off on his travels. Well, like Mr Atkins said, you can't live on half-wages, can you? That's why he let them all go.'

Lilith was only supposed to be finding out whether Mrs Bell was expecting to cook a formal dinner for some two dozen guests in seven days' time, but this was too tempting a development to ignore. 'How inventive of him,' she said, stepping out of her remit without a second thought.

'Mr Atkins was full of them schemes. Fill a person's head with riches, he could. It was a shock when we thought the master was coming back last month. Pricked his bubble. Daresay that's when he started planning to scarper.' Mrs Bell's face settled into brooding lines.

'Very likely,' said Lilith. She wondered if she could capitalise on the cook's sense of maltreatment to find out about Mrs Gunn. She could well believe the majority of the house had not been cleaned for several months, but this sitting room looked to have been used until relatively recently. 'This is a pleasant room,' she said, glancing around. 'It must have made a great deal of extra work for you without a housekeeper these last weeks.'

'Her? She's no loss. Giving herself airs. Telling me what to cook as if I hadn't been doing it all my life. No better than the rest of us when she came to it though, was she?'

'No?' asked Lilith.

Sadly, her gently inviting tone was lost in Mrs Bell's gin-fuelled sense of injustice. The cook grabbed for the table and made a jabbing motion with a pudgy forefinger. 'You tell the master all this housemaiding ain't what I'm used to. Nor the half-wages neither. I'm only staying on to oblige while he's got the young gentlemen in the house. I'm back off to my brother at the Wagon and Horses after that, no matter how much he offers me.'

Lilith schooled her expression to one of polite sympathy. 'That is most understandable. I'm sure you will not find Mr Makepeace lacking in gratitude.'

* * *

'You have wrought a miracle!' Edward's face filled with incredulous delight. Just so had he looked that first day when he'd found a minute piece of pottery in the excavation. 'I can barely believe it. When is she going?'

'As soon as you hand over a farewell purse, I imagine,' said Lilith, amused. She hadn't liked Mrs Bell, but her cooking must be grim indeed to provoke this much of a reaction. 'I wish I could take the credit for her decision, but it was nothing to do with me.'

'I shall break open the strongbox immediately. How much?'

'For a cook? I would have thought five guineas, plus the carriage of her worldly goods to her brother's inn.'

'Splendid. I shall tell Kerr to . . . ' He stopped. 'I shall make enquiries myself about a new cook.'

'You will not get one by next week. Woods, however, has reminded me of our own cook's niece in town. Mary has assisted Cook for several years, but she is walking out with the second footman and is looking for her own kitchen. She would do admirably here, and Joshua would likewise be an asset to you. I will write to Ben about them today, if you like? Meanwhile I believe you need a plan of campaign. You cannot wait for your secretary to return to his senses. Your next step, I suggest, is to enquire at all the Newmarket hotels to ascertain if their cooks or their function rooms have been engaged by Kerr on your behalf. A perusal of the ledger may also throw up a payment or a retainer.'

He nodded, his gaze straying regretfully to the window. She could see what he really wanted to be doing was joining the men at the dyke. He sighed resolutely and turned back to her. 'What do you say to bundling up the ledgers, the strongbox and the letters, and going through them in your sitting room at Furze House? I should check the inns without delay. Ricky can divide the task with me.'

Lilith saw any chance of searching Mr Kerr's pocketbook for mention of Flint disappearing. 'Certainly,' she replied. 'A little scholarly application and we will untangle this coil in no time.'

14

'Nothing,' said Ned some time later, coming into Lilith's saloon with Ricky. She was at the table with Catherine and Dacre, ledgers and correspondence spread out in front of them.

'Nothing at all?' she asked.

He shook his head. 'None of the cooks have been approached and all the larger hotels say they cannot accommodate a dinner for two dozen at such short notice. Not only is there a fair next week, with many guests booked, Rutland is holding his own dinner at Cheveley shortly before, so the strain on their dining rooms with members of the Quality in the town will be considerable.'

Lilith sorted through the correspondence. 'Yes, you have been invited to Cheveley. I assume your secretary accepted for you, for his Grace is delighted you can attend and is looking forward to yours. Does Kerr hate you very much, Edward?'

He gave a short laugh. 'I have never thought so before. He has always seemed devoid of emotion, wouldn't you say, Ricky? There is no help for it, I shall have to write to everyone to cancel. Bringing a chef from town would be ruinous.'

'Not necessarily,' said Lilith slowly.

'No, it really would be.'

Lilith and Catherine were looking at each other in silent communication. Ned eyed them warily.

Catherine nodded. 'I think so, yes. Eleven dishes, do you think? Or thirteen? Is the kitchen well equipped?'

'Woods will know. He can act as butler if we find him a coat. Footmen! Where are we ever going to find enough? I hope you get a good response tomorrow, Edward.'

The conversation seemed to have taken off without him. 'Are you suggesting *Catherine* cooks for my dinner?' he said, trying to keep the incredulity out of his voice.

'Oh, yes!' said Ricky, his face joyous.

'Not without me there,' said Dacre grimly.

Catherine laid a hand on Dacre's arm. 'I will be in the kitchen, aproned and mob-capped and no one will refer to me by name. You will have to go to Bury St Edmunds for wine, Edward.'

'It is a gentlemen's dinner, Nicholas,' said Lilith. 'Have you ever been to such a one where you would even see the chef, let alone recognise them the next day?'

'Please,' said Ned. 'Please can someone explain?'

'Catherine is willing to cook, but she had a problem in London,' said Lilith after a moment of silence. 'That is why Nicholas is concerned for her.' She drew a shallow breath. 'It is her own fault for being so very lovely. Beauty often attracts unwelcome admirers.'

There was something more here, something they weren't telling him. He let it go. There was too much else to worry about. 'I am more grateful than I can say, Catherine. My scholars leave on Monday, so I will endeavour to shift Mrs Bell out of Ditton Place at the same time. I daresay the agency can come up with a temporary cook to feed the household if necessary. You must order what provisions you like, Catherine, but I do not advise viewing the kitchen until after Mrs Bell has left.'

'Hester tells me we will need to get in to scrub it as soon as she leaves,' said Lilith. 'I daresay the women here will all help. Meanwhile I have found a list of your previous servants and what they were paid. It seems very generous. There is no mention of half-pay.' She hesitated, her hand hovering over the ledger in front of her. 'I have also found an entry that I do not understand. Is Kerr accustomed to write everything down as regards finances, or does he merely enter what is left over after daily expenses are taken out?'

Ned frowned. 'He writes down

everything, as far as I am aware. He prides himself on his thoroughness and efficiency. Why do you ask?'

Lilith raised her clear gaze to his. 'Because not all the money Benedict gave you for my tuition has been entered.'

'I passed the roll of banknotes to Kerr exactly as your brother left it with me.'

'Then he must have kept some back for the journey, perhaps.' She ran her finger down the neat lines of writing. 'You do seem to run quite an expensive establishment. A gross of best beeswax candles seems extravagant, and it is quite unnecessary to bring down hams and geese from town when the local butcher would supply them more cheaply.'

Ned felt his jaw drop. 'We didn't. Atkins made a point of saying we had arrived with no notice and Mrs Bell had had to do her best with what little there was in the house. It was mutton, so far as I could tell. I haven't seen goose since we left town.'

'We didn't bring candles either,' added Ricky. 'I had to beg working ones from Peter the first night and most were stubs.'

'Kerr must have ordered them to be delivered later.' Ned looked at the disbelief on their faces. 'What? What are you suggesting?'

There was sympathy in Lilith's eyes. 'That your secretary might be as much of a rogue as your butler, but rather more clever about it.'

Ned took a moment to assimilate this. 'You think Kerr has falsified the accounts and kept the money for himself? Why? He never spends half his salary as it is. He dresses plainly, does not drink to excess, he has never appeared to have any personal ambition, no grand scheme to aim at.'

'Maybe it was to send money to his mother? To make himself appear more successful than is actually the case? Oh!'

'What is it?'

'His mother's letters were crossed and crossed again.'

'What of it? Do you think there is anything in them? You will have to read them if so. I could barely make out one word in seven.'

'If Kerr can read them sufficient to answer, he must also have been able to read your sister-in-law's letter, the one announcing her arrival in town.'

Ned put his head in his hands. 'I am living in a nightmare. That makes no sense. Why would he conceal that?'

'I can't imagine, but I think the time has come to find out,' replied Lilith. 'What do you actually know of your secretary?'

He exchanged a look with Ricky and made a helpless gesture. 'That he is a Scot. That he is hard-working. That he has rigid principals and no vices.'

'In my experience,' drawled Dacre, 'when a man seems too good to be true, there's a pile of bones in the closet he'd rather we didn't find out about.'

'Do you mean *Kerr* might be

dishonest?' said Ricky, his voice rising in disbelief.

'It is just that he doesn't seem to have been acting in your brother's best interests recently,' said Lilith apologetically.

'But . . . ' Ricky fell silent, frowning to himself.

'There is also the discrepancy between Mr Thornley's notions of the cost of an Egyptian expedition and your own,' Lilith said.

Ned looked up. 'What in the world has Thornley to do with anything?'

'He says the porters out there exist on pennies. You told me they were expensive.'

'They are,' said Ned. He cast his mind back to the summer. 'Though you wouldn't know it to look at them.' The words tasted bitter in his mouth. 'How arrogant of me not to ask, not to check.' He stared at the ledger which had now assumed the aspect of a man-eating hydra. 'You are suggesting Kerr has been lying to me in order to send my money to his mother — and I am such a trusting fool that I believed him?'

Lilith put her hand on his. 'I am sorry.'

Catherine rose. 'Nicholas, can you help me downstairs for a moment? Ricky, I wonder if you would be very kind and finish telling my daughter that story about the Romans that you were acting out yesterday for her and her friends. They are in the yard helping with the laundry. I feel sure your tales would make working the mangle go faster.'

He was being left alone to get over Kerr's deceit. He looked at Lilith's hand, still resting on his. He tried to speak, but the words couldn't get through the bile in his throat. He had never felt more of a failure.

★   ★   ★

Lilith couldn't bear it. Edward's trust had been shattered. He was hurting. 'Tell me about your mother,' she said.

He looked up, startled out of wherever his thoughts were taking him. 'My mother?'

'Yes. I am sick of puzzles and double-dealing. I want to talk of normal things for a change. Was your mother as gentle-natured as Ricky? I feel sure she must have been.'

He gave a small laugh and sat back. 'Very much so. Unlike my father. They were most unsuited. He was tough and unimaginative, enjoyed good living and country pursuits. He had no concept of frailty. I do not believe he had a day's illness in his life. Henry and I took after him in physique. Ricky favoured my mother. My father could not understand him at all. Ricky rides well, but not to hounds. He is a good shot, but hates to kill. He would rather read than play cards.'

'Another scholar, in other words,' said Lilith.

'You may imagine how that exasperated my father. Five years ago in the middle of winter, he came back from an afternoon's shooting and caught Ricky teaching the boot boy to read. God knows what he saw in it, but he decided Ricky needed toughening up and marched him out just as he was — without greatcoat or muffler — to the gamekeeper's hut in the woods. He told him not to come home for twenty-four hours. That night there was a blizzard. My mother was never strong. She ate little for dinner and retired early. I slipped straightaway upstairs to tell her I would fetch Ricky home, but to my horror she had gone out herself to find him. I discovered her half-dead in a snowdrift, carried her home, returned for Ricky and got him back in scarcely better condition. We lost my mother. I bullied Ricky back to health.'

That was when he had made the promise. That was why he set so much store by it. Oh, Edward. 'And you have been looking after him ever since,' she said softly. She clasped his hand. 'I am so sorry.'

'The horror of that night. It is not something I will ever forget. I never forgave my father. I would have moved to Ditton Place immediately but my work and contacts were all in London and there was Ricky to take care of. I had to ensure he got the education he deserved. I told my father that as I now had Mama's money, I would go to the London house and get my brother into Westminster and out of his sight. It was a civilised breach. We used the town house, only visiting Hampshire at Christmas. In the eyes of the world, there would not seem to have been a falling-out at all. We met occasionally at social events, my father set my marriage contract in train . . . but, as I told you, he had his seizure at the house party where I was supposed to make the offer. It had been his scheme. I let it drop without regret.'

Lilith absorbed all this in silence. Edward stirred. 'We should not be sitting so close.'

'It seems unexceptional. Don't you like it?'

'Very much, but we are not chaperoned.'

'Intelligent people do not need antiquated rules. I trust you not to take advantage. Contact is comforting.' She looked at their clasped hands. 'All this time, you have had no one to talk to about your mother, no one to help shoulder the burden. That is bravery. Carrying on. Doing what you must. You are a good man.'

He gave a bark of laughter. 'You would not say that if you had felt the dislike directed at me in the Three Blackbirds this afternoon. I have been remiss and failed those I had a duty of care to.'

She smiled up at him. 'You will address some of the wrongs tomorrow if your former servants return.' She paused, thoughtful. 'Though I do not think we can now believe your secretary's list of wages. What do you intend to do about him?'

'Wait until he is better, then dismiss him. I cannot throw him out of the house ill.'

It was in Lilith's mind that Edward would now not object to her reading Kerr's correspondence. She could do it easily on the grounds of finding out in what other ways he had been robbing Edward. It was even stronger in her mind that she couldn't deceive him one moment more. She knew there was nothing harmful in this man.

'I should like tea,' she said. 'I will go and ask Catherine. Would you like to see my sketch of Ricky? It will give you time to frame a diplomatic opinion if you look at it while I am out of the room.' She stood and opened the book at the right page, then went slowly downstairs.

She had just finished asking Catherine and Nicholas for permission to tell Edward about the connection between Kerr and Flint when they heard feet thundering down the stairs. Edward erupted into Catherine's sitting room, brandishing Lilith's sketchbook.

'When did you do this?'

They turned surprised faces to him. 'On the day of my arrival,' said Lilith. 'That is Mrs Smith, the lady upstairs with the baby.'

'It is also Mrs Gunn, my house-keeper.'

Lilith stared at him. A false name she could understand, but the woman had been turned off because she was expecting a child. No! That had not been Edward! He could not have done such a thing. Lilith's heart threatened to fracture.

Edward was still gripping the sketch-book. 'Will she come back to Ditton Place? Is she fit enough? May I see her?'

Then it hadn't been him. He could not be acting a part here. Overcome with relief, Lilith looked at Catherine. Catherine shrugged.

'Edward . . . ' Lilith moistened her lips. 'Mrs Smith — Gunn — says she had to leave her position because she was expecting a child.'

He looked blankly at her, then his face grew wrathful. 'Atkins! By God, he took too much on himself. But Mrs Gunn had worked for us many years. She should have known I would help. Why did she not write to me in London?'

'I did,' said a voice from the doorway.

Lilith whirled around. Mrs Smith stood there, one hand on the jamb, supporting herself. 'I wrote and received a severance letter.'

'Mrs Gunn, it really is you! I swear I did not dismiss you. I would not do such a thing. I had no idea you were even in distress.'

'The letter was in your name.'

Lilith watched the rage chase across Edward's face. She had been right. This was a decent man. 'Kerr!' he choked. 'Blast his Calvinistic morals! How dare he not ask my views first? Please tell me it was not in my writing? My dear Mrs Gunn, it is so good to see you.' He hurried forward as he spoke and helped her to a chair.

'It was not in your writing,' she said, and smiled. 'How are you, Mr Edward?'

'So very much better for finding you. However did you come to such a pass?'

She gave a strained smile. 'There is no fool like an old fool, as the proverb goes. A handsome face, a little flattery, a glass of wine . . . '

'We will no longer think of it, unless I may be of assistance horsewhipping the scoundrel?'

'No, he treated me fairly, within his own code, until near the end when I saw he cared more about his position than he ever had for mine.'

'Then will you come back to Ditton Place? As soon as you are recovered from your lying in, that is? We are in desperate need of your touch at the helm once more.'

She hesitated. 'I do not think that will be possible. Not while Mr Atkins is there. I'm sorry, but . . . '

'Atkins is dead.'

At this intelligence, Mrs Gunn's pallor became even more pronounced.

'Then there is no longer any bar. Forgive me, he played me for a fool, but it is still a shock. I will tell you. He had not long arrived before he started to pay me rather more than friendly attention. I see now that it was to get me on his side, but at the time I was flattered.'

'Blackguard.'

'Shortly after you left, we received a letter telling us we were all to be on half-wages until you returned.'

'I did not approve any such order.'

'Again, it was in your name. I thought it strange as it had never happened before, but I had other things to worry about. I wrote to you to explain my predicament. I received a severance letter by return. I was so shocked, so very shocked. Mr Atkins seemed sympathetic. He could not offer marriage, he said, because he had an estranged wife. He intimated that my plight was partly my own fault for tempting him — which I swear I did not. Finally, he said I could stay in my suite and you would never know, but he would have to turn off the staff for fear they would talk.'

'So you had all the work of the house!' cried Lilith. 'What a vile creature.'

'I have known easier times,' admitted Mrs Gunn. 'About a month ago we received word that you would be returning. This frightened Mr Atkins so much that he said I must go. I found refuge with Mr Locke and his sister . . . '

'What?' cried Edward. 'Is Locke nearby?'

'In Cheveley. Did you not know? His sister has long had a small cottage in the village.'

'No, Kerr did not tell me, and to my eternal shame I did not ask. Being absorbed in my work is no excuse. Let me tell you I am becoming heartily sick of myself. Is Locke well?'

'Why yes, though his sister is very frail. They took me in without question, such old friends as we are, but it has been a strain. Mr Locke's annuity had been cut . . . '

'Not by me.'

' . . . and I only had my small savings. Mr Locke's sister is older than him, but so kind. She would not hear of me leaving until word reached us of Furze House. That seemed the ideal place for me, so I set off. I did not realise how close I was to my time. I have since sent Miss Locke word I was safely delivered, and that I have named the child Jane after her.'

'Will you give me Locke's address? I must visit and make reparation. I will need a new secretary too. After what I have learnt today, I am not sure I can bear to have Kerr in the house until he is recovered enough for me to dismiss him.'

Lilith's heart was almost painfully full, listening to this vindication of Edward being all she'd thought him.

Nicholas cleared his throat. 'There might be a problem with that.'

But Edward frowned, deep in

thought. 'Wait. Atkins was robbing me by keeping the servants' wages, but Kerr had robbed me *first*, by putting them on half-pay and keeping the remainder for himself. Furthermore, Atkins knew Kerr was aware Mrs Gunn was not in residence and that he had clearly not informed me. I thought he sounded odd when he requested a private interview. He didn't really want one — it was a threat, knowing Kerr was listening.'

'You believe he was blackmailing Kerr?' said Nicholas.

Edward nodded. 'He had to have been. Atkins would have wanted a fat purse in exchange for going quietly. Yet there was no money on him, nor in the bags. I begin to wonder whether he fell or was pushed.'

Nicholas said deliberately, 'Or even whether Kerr slugged him quietly in his own room and disposed of his body in your ditch.'

'Packing the bags himself and taking them later? It could be. It must have given him a bad few hours when Peter Swann was so rigorously on duty in the hall and then took the keys to bed with him. Can we prove any of this? I would give Kerr in charge as soon as may be.'

'That,' said Nicholas again, 'is something we need to discuss.'

And Lilith would have to tell Edward she'd been deceiving him. She rose. 'Mrs Gunn, I feel sure you should be resting. I wonder if you might help us with one thing? If I give you a list of former servants at Ditton Place, might you be able to tell us what their wages were as far as you remember? Mr Makepeace is to interview some of them tomorrow and we believe his secretary did not enter the salaries correctly in the accounts.'

'With pleasure.' Mrs Gunn eased herself upright. 'Oh, if I had not forgotten!' she said, appalled at her lapse. 'I came down for a little warmed milk, but I heard Mr Edward and could not ignore him.'

Catherine chuckled. 'I'll see to it. I

shouldn't worry. Babies are more adaptable than you think.'

'I'll help you upstairs,' said Lilith.

'It is very good to have found you again,' said Edward with a smile.

'And may I really have the position back?'

'With my heartfelt gratitude. Engage a personal maid for yourself and the child, and I will add her to the household wage list.'

Lilith lent Mrs Gunn an unobtrusive hand, keenly aware that with every word Edward said he was making it more difficult for her to admit to her duplicity.

15

'Mrs Gunn has told me the amounts,' said Lilith, entering her saloon to find Edward and Nicholas going through the ledgers again. 'She says there is a true list in the bureau in the housekeeper's sitting room. I will look for it in the morning,'

Edward looked up, his eyes rueful. 'Thank you,' he said. 'I am sorry. I will be appalling company this evening. This does not make for good reading. I am ashamed it has been happening under my eyes. I can think of nothing except how soon I may dismiss Kerr.'

'Unfortunately, that's the last thing we'd like you to do,' said Nicholas, trying for the third time to broach the subject.

Edward frowned. 'I beg your pardon?'

His face was open and puzzled. Lilith swallowed and sat down on the sofa, fixing her eyes on her clasped hands. This was going to be dreadful. Resolutely, she repeated what Kerr had said when he'd been semi-conscious. 'I am so sorry, Edward. I couldn't tell you because . . . because . . . '

'Because you thought I might be involved too. I thought we had a better understanding.' His voice was bitter.

Tears gathered in her eyes. She was utterly unable to look at him.

'Lilith was right,' said Nicholas. 'Personal consideration is irrelevant in such a case. None of us knew you from Adam, and the number of gentlemen Flint has sunk his lures into is frightening. Think, man. With your brother visiting Wardour Street . . . '

Edward pushed his chair back violently. Lilith felt the sofa dip as he sat next to her. His forearm, firm and capable, swam into her blurred vision. 'I was hasty,' he said, taking her tightly clasped hands in his own. 'I apologise.'

She forced herself to meet his eyes, forced herself to face the hurt in them.

'I couldn't tell you, Edward. It was Catherine's life at risk.'

'I understand. I am a brute and do not deserve such friends.' He brought her hand up and brushed a kiss across her fingers. 'Did you find anything in Kerr's room?'

The kiss felt like forgiveness, branded on her skin, spreading and tingling through her body. The warmth of his breath set her trembling. She wanted the whole desperate, sordid tangle to be cleared away so she could concentrate on what she felt for Edward and what he might feel for her. 'There was nothing about Flint,' she said, amazed to hear her voice through the tumultuous beating of her heart. 'I had hopes of a locked box, but it contained only coins, signet rings, heather — presumably from home — and a rough pebble. I haven't looked through his pocketbook.'

'Signet rings?' Edward frowned. 'I have never seen Kerr wear a ring.'

'There were two of them. Oh, do you

think they might have a family crest? I never thought of that.'

But Nicholas had sat up alertly. 'Lilith, what sort of a pebble?'

She met his eyes in surprise. 'Whitish, misshapen, but smooth.'

He bit off an exclamation, left the room, and reappeared a few moments later with Catherine. 'I'm sorry about your sauce, my love, but tell them of our shadowy friend's peculiar and very particular business practice.'

Catherine opened her hand. On her palm lay an irregular smooth white pebble, streaks of black showing through the surface. 'Was the stone you found like this?'

Lilith nodded. 'It was similar, yes. What is it for?'

'It is a receipt,' said Catherine in a level voice. 'A token, given in return for a blackmail payment to show the debt has been paid and will not be called in again. This one belonged to my father. It is a nodule of flint.'

'Flint?' For a moment Lilith was

puzzled. Then she understood. 'Oh, a flint from Flint. I see. You think Kerr had been sent it in return for finding out about you?'

Nicholas shook his head. 'That is not how Flint operates. He learns a secret, demands blackmail money in return for not making the secret public, and then sends the token once the money has been paid. Sometimes he sets a task instead of asking for money.'

Lilith frowned. 'Then that means . . . '

'That means,' said Edward, an intent frown on his face, 'that Kerr has *already* done something to be blackmailed over and has already paid the price for it to be wiped out. Presumably with my embezzled money.'

'That would be my deduction,' said Nicholas. 'If he has now been told to look for Catherine in Newmarket and report back, it means Flint still has a hold over him. He must have done something else that he doesn't want made public.'

'Continued to rob me, probably.'

'Undoubtedly, but it seems unlikely Flint would know about it. The point I am trying to make is that my friends and I would be very grateful if you could see your way to *not* dismissing your secretary and reporting him to the nearest authorities, but instead could keep a close watch on him that we might trace a thread back to Flint. We do, most urgently, need to know who Flint is.'

'You want me to keep Kerr in my house? A man I know to have been embezzling, and suspect of murdering my butler? I won't do it. Nobody could.'

'Flint is a killer,' said Nicholas. 'He hides in shadows and is ruling London by fear. He slits the throats of people like Nash's builders who oppose him. He flogs vulnerable, anonymous women for his own gratification and drops their bodies in the Thames. He's the one we want. Donald Kerr is a very petty fellow indeed beside him.'

Edward was silent for a long

moment. Catherine murmured to Nicholas and slipped away. Edward looked up. 'What would you have me do?'

'Continue as you are. Search for any scrap of information that might point to Flint. Otherwise leave Kerr alone, but keep a watch on him.'

'You can be sure of that,' said Edward bitterly. He took a deep breath. 'Very well.'

'He will have to regain consciousness first,' said Lilith. 'The doctor thinks he must have an idiosyncrasy for laudanum to still be in a stupor.'

'If that is the case, I wish I had fed him the whole bottle,' muttered Edward.

★ ★ ★

Ricky was quiet in the carriage back to Ditton Place. Hardly surprising, thought Ned, taking a wager with himself that his brother would barely manage half an hour's conversation with the scholars before his eyes were closing. It was a healthy tiredness though, a far cry from the drug-induced exhaustion of recent months. Today he was simply full of good food and had worn himself out re-enacting Roman history to an appreciative audience of children, grooms, stable hands and passing cronies of the gardener.

They had taken the decision that they would not tell him yet of Kerr's link to Flint. Ricky knew the secretary had been defrauding Ned, but he was so very partisan on his brother's behalf that it was safer to keep him in the dark about the rest, for fear of him angrily letting slip to Kerr that the Pool was on to him.

The Pool. As Ned handed his hat and gloves absently to Peter, he considered what he had learnt of this dedicated band of otherwise ordinary gentlemen. It was Lord Fitzgilbert who was leading the hunt for Flint. That same amusing, intelligent man who had made friendly conversation the morning he had brought Lilith's tuition money. A gentleman with a political social life, estates to oversee, bailiffs to talk to, tenants to keep happy — and still he privately checked leads to Flint, collated information, sent out agents. A man in charge of a quiet, clandestine operation designed to make London safe for all classes, not just his own.

And that man was Lilith's brother. Those were the ideals she would have grown up with. No wonder she put duty above self. Ned was uncomfortably aware that he fell short of those ideals in almost every possible way. Well then, he would redeem himself a little by searching Kerr's rooms.

Ferris, however, met him at Kerr's door with the news that the secretary was waking more often, though he didn't seem much better than when they'd brought him in.

'He's certainly making enough noise,' said Ned, standing in the doorway and looking at the groaning, sweating man in the bed. 'What's your opinion?'

Ferris, along with Chilcott, now knew about Kerr's financial irregularities. 'It seems a shame to deprive the young gentlemen of their rest,' he said woodenly. His eyes strayed to the laudanum bottle.

'I agree. Let him wake during the day, not at night.'

'I am sure the sleep will do him a power of good, sir.'

* * *

The next morning, Lilith arrived while they were all still at breakfast. Ned caught a glimpse of her skirts whisking past the breakfast parlour door and was visited by such a piercing pleasure that he inadvertently allowed Peter to serve him with a slice of beef and a portion of kidneys.

'I could wish my scholars were as eager to learn as yours,' murmured Thornley. He cast a speculative look sideways at his host. 'An apt pupil, is she?'

'Miss Fitzgilbert has a mind of the highest order,' said Ned in repressive tones.

'Oh, bad luck,' said Thornley sympathetically. 'She has a mighty persistent maid too. Coming out with us this morning?'

'I wish I could. I have to interview my former servants. Perhaps later.'

Thornley nodded. Ned discovered what he was eating, told Peter to return it to the kitchen with the comment that when he wanted to eat boot leather he would request Ferris to remove the nails from it first, and went in search of Lilith.

She was in the housekeeper's room with Woods. She had found the list Mrs Gunn had mentioned and was making a fair copy of it while Woods and Hester between them directed the maids to clean the small set of interconnected rooms and make them ready to receive Mrs Gunn again.

'I see no reason for you to keep from your former servants that she will be returning when she is recovered,' said Lilith. 'As soon as the news permeates to the village, I imagine your reception there will be a lot less frosty.'

'In my experience it will reach there in roughly two minutes flat. I am more worried about the news reaching Kerr's ears. As soon as it does, he will know I have found him out.'

'Mr Kerr appears not to talk to the servants,' said Woods, keeping an eye through the door on the maids engaged in dusting the bedroom. 'Miss Fitzgilbert has entered her in your new list as Mrs Smith, to start in a month's time. She will be assumed to have been found by the registry office.'

'Meanwhile, this will be a useful suite for Catherine to use while organising your dinner,' said Lilith. She finished her copying and handed the sheet of paper to him. 'Oh,' she said, looking past him, 'you have another medicine chest in here. Goodness, what a handsome piece. You would be able to doctor the whole village with it.'

Ned smiled. 'I believe Mrs Gunn did just that. She was much liked.'

Lilith wrinkled her brow in the intelligent way he had come to recognise. 'Then why is there a second cabinet in your secretary's study? Some ten inches high, double-fronted.' She shaped it with her hands.

'That is Kerr's own travelling medicine chest,' replied Ned. 'It never leaves his side when we go away. We have often been grateful for it.' That was another puzzle. Why had Kerr looked after them so well? Presumably to make sure of keeping his position.

There was a tiny silence. He caught up with what he'd said. *It never leaves his side*. That could be where a clue to Flint might lie!

Lilith swivelled to her maid. 'Hester, in the medicine cabinet at home, do I remember a shallow drawer where Mama used to keep the family receipts?'

'That's right enough, Miss Lilith.'

'We've time to check now, if Kerr is

still asleep,' said Ned grimly.

Within a matter of minutes, Ferris had silently extracted the keys from the bedchamber and Lilith was opening the travelling medicine chest.

'Wasn't taking any risk on any of you catching anything in them foreign places, was he?' remarked Hester, surveying the contents. 'I've never seen one so well stocked. Regular apothecary's shop. White arsenic, look, and opium and goodness knows what else. Whatever does he want with all this stuff, Mr Ferris?'

'Abroad is a shocking place for the belly, Miss Hepple.'

Hester continued to look at the chest in a jaundiced fashion. 'You never thought, Mr Ferris, that he might have caused some of that himself?'

Lilith had pulled out the drawer of receipts, written in Kerr's neat hand, and was flicking through them quickly. 'This isn't a remedy,' she said, handing a much folded list of names to Ned.

He frowned. 'It is a collection of

members of the ton,' he said, mystified. 'Several have marks against them. Why would he keep this here?'

'Perhaps it is an account of prospective households, should you not rise to sufficient importance in your profession,' suggested Lilith with a trace of mischief.

'Hardly.' He winced as he saw Lord Hare's name. 'Lord Hare, for instance, has a seat in Leicestershire and rarely leaves it. It was Lady Isabel Hare to whom I was to make an offer.' He flushed, feeling all the awkwardness attendant on a shamefully welcome escape. He had gone unwillingly to the house party, propelled in large measure by the prospect of making a settled home for Ricky. Then his father had his seizure and all plans were dropped. It was as well. The marriage would only ever have been one of polite convenience. Lady Isabel was pleasant, well-bred and respectably endowed, but she wasn't . . .

The revelation struck him like a tree

he had once seen consumed by lightning. Vivid brightness lit up his mind. Magnesium fire tingled over his whole body. Wonder engulfed him, as a man might experience on viewing the dawn of the universe.

Eminently suitable though Lady Isabel had been, she wasn't Lilith.

He stared at the list of names. This time last week, he hadn't known Lilith. Now, he couldn't imagine life without her. He could feel her watching him, could picture exactly the sympathy in her gaze. How was he even to go about courting such a woman? He, who had failed so utterly in all the principles she held dear. *Breathe, Ned. This too shall pass.* He made himself focus on Kerr's neat writing.

And straightened abruptly. 'Wait . . . these are all the gentlemen at Lord Hare's house party, the one at which my father died!'

'Was Kerr present?'

'Yes, naturally, we were expecting there would be a lot of business to attend to. As indeed there was, but not the sort we expected. I cannot think of any reason for Kerr to have made this list, or to have kept it.'

Lilith held out her hand. 'It's all we have. Let me copy it while you interview your staff and we can study the names later. I will undertake to put everything back as we found it. Kerr will have no idea we were ever interested.'

⋆　⋆　⋆

By the time Ned could get out to the site, it was afternoon. He had half the Ditton Place servants back again. He had ridden over to call on Locke and assure him that the annuity would be reinstated. 'He cannot leave his sister though,' he said to Lilith as they strolled towards the dyke. In the distance they could hear the sound of the scholars' voices. 'I will have to see what the registry office can supply. Will you interview the applicants with me? I shall be wholly at sea otherwise.'

'Would Woods not be better?'

'Left to myself I would be tempted to let him deal with the whole. If you are there, I will have an incentive to carry out the business properly, to redeem myself in your eyes.' *He was making a cake of himself. He knew it. He didn't seem able to stop. That revelation of earlier was still seared into him.*

'How foolish. Why would my opinion matter?'

'Because . . . because . . . ' He looked at her helplessly, wondering if his mind would ever work properly again.

Her colour heightened. Ned hoped that might be an encouraging sign. 'Tell me about the dyke,' she said, changing the subject. 'Will you get everything you wish done before Mr Thornley and his men return to London?'

Something I can answer at last. 'This site is a continuous project. I do what I can when I am here and write up the results ready for next time. In truth, this week was more of a . . . ' At the sound of running footsteps behind them he broke off. 'Yes, Peter?' he said with resignation. 'What is it now?'

'His Grace, sir. The Duke of Rutland, sir. Mr Woods told me to fetch you quick sharp.'

Ned sighed. 'It seems you are destined to resume your wandering through my library rather than my excavation,' he said. *And he was destined never to get a proper word with her alone, away from mysteries and explanations and shame.*

'I can think of worse places to be,' replied Lilith.

They returned to the house to be confronted by a very handsome phaeton, drawn by a pair of beautifully matched greys, and driven by . . .

'Your Grace,' said Ned at once, bowing low to the duchess. 'How delightful to see you at Ditton Place. Might I say what an enchanting picture you present?'

'I should hope so,' remarked the Duke of Rutland from his seat next to his lady, 'considering what I paid for them. Dacre-matched, you know.'

Dacre . . . 'Is that so?' said Ned smoothly. 'I dined with Dacre the other day and he was telling me about his new venture. These are a beautiful pair.'

'Lilith!' exclaimed the duchess. She seemed highly diverted. 'Lilith Fitzgilbert! So this is where you retired to. Whatever are you doing in Cambridgeshire? My dear girl, you will be weary of it within a week. Tell me at once, is it true?'

Was what true? Ned continued to talk to the duke, but listened with half an ear as Lilith moved gracefully towards the side of the phaeton.

'Good day, your Grace,' she said. 'I am taking the opportunity of Mr Makepeace's excavation to learn about antiquities. It is a fascinating subject.'

'Don't be provoking, Lilith.'

'I assure you it is why I am here.'

'Tiresome creature. Is your brother in Newmarket? You must come and dine. Where are you staying?'

'Benedict is busy in London. I am staying at Furze House, the boarding house for gentlewomen that he and some friends are establishing in New-market. It needs a great deal of refurbishment. Between that and the antiquarian studies, I have little time to miss the capital.'

'Then you shall come and dine tomorrow and I will tell you all the news you have missed.'

'I regret, ma'am, that I am not socialising at present.'

The Duchess of Rutland gave a crow of laughter. 'So it *was* true. How too enterprising of you, my dear. Your mother would have been exceedingly proud. You must tell me how you managed it tomorrow night.'

'But I . . . '

'Cheveley is not London. A small gathering in the country will do no harm at all. Mr Makepeace, I charge you to escort Miss Fitzgilbert to dine with us at Cheveley tomorrow.'

Ned bowed. 'Your wish is naturally my command.'

'You have very pretty manners. Well, I can't keep the horses standing any longer. We thought we would drive this way so I could show my dear Rutland how well his present suits me, but it is too cold to be out for long. Until tomorrow.'

'What was that about?' Ned asked as they watched the phaeton disappear back towards Cheveley.

Lilith eyed him. 'The duchess is well known for her hospitality. It is her desire that I should join the dinner guests tomorrow. I do hope you are not the sort of gentleman who listens to private conversations?'

Not until now. 'I wouldn't dream of it,' replied Ned.

16

'I knew we'd need the fine gowns,' remarked Hester as she arranged Lilith's hair the following day.

'As ever, Hester, you were entirely right. It seems even when I look forward to a few weeks of pure study, I am to be thwarted.' The morning had not been entirely wasted. She had received a letter from town saying the cook and footman would arrive early next week and she had discovered that when Edward put his mind to something, like learning what to ask of unknown domestics, he did it thoroughly. Ditton Place would soon be fully staffed, lacking only a butler and a housekeeper. Mrs Gunn wouldn't return until after Kerr had been dealt with. Another incentive to trace his connection to Flint as fast as possible.

'Now then, Miss Lilith,' said Hester,

'your mother always said it was necessary to mix in society before you could change it.'

'Mama was a learned social reformer. I am . . . I don't know what I am.'

Edward, however, when he called for her, seemed to know exactly what she was. 'Charming and elegant,' he said.

'Thank you. I should prefer to be wind-blown and ankle deep in the dirt in your ditch. However, social duty is social duty.' She looked a query as Ferris appeared behind his master.

Edward smiled. 'Kerr has been very noisy and unsettled and difficult to deal with today. As Ferris has born the brunt of it, I have given him the evening off and the promise of a decent dinner in the kitchen here. Woods very nobly offered to keep an eye on Kerr.'

'If you'll come this way, Mr Ferris,' said Hester, very formal.

Ferris inclined his head. 'Certainly, Miss Hepple.'

They moved in a stately fashion down the hallway. Lilith looked at

Edward, round-eyed in surprise. 'Goodness, are they . . . ?'

'I make it a rule never to ask.' There was a lurking smile in his eyes as he proffered his arm. 'Your carriage awaits.'

Lilith laid a hand on his sleeve, feeling absurdly shy all of a sudden. In the carriage, as he settled himself next to her, she was aware of his understated strength, the length of his limbs, his profile as he turned to her with a smile.

'Do you know,' he said, 'this is almost the first time we have been completely alone.'

'Apart from the first day when you showed me the dyke, and the time you came to dine at Furze House and were shown into the saloon, and when . . . '

He sighed. 'Are you always so exact?'

'Invariably. Also, there are a limited number of responses one can make to a remark like that.'

He chuckled and possessed himself of her hand. 'It is the first time we are alone and likely to be undisturbed and

291

it feels very comfortable.'

'It does. I feel safe, and yet . . . ' *And yet suddenly not safe at all.*

'As if, perhaps, we were on the brink of something new?'

Lilith's heart beat faster. What was he leading up to? 'Perhaps,' she temporised.

His thumb described a lazy circle on her gloved palm. 'Is it something you feel you might like?'

'I . . . I had not considered . . . that is, I had not thought . . . ' But she had, she realised. She had been thinking it, deep down, for quite a while. She was thinking it now. Warmth filled her. She looked up at him. 'I believe I might like it, yes.'

He smiled. 'I'm glad.'

She waited, hardly daring to breathe, but the carriage moved through the dusk in silence. 'Is that it?' she asked after a moment.

'I hadn't thought very much further,' he admitted. 'I'm not sure I expected you to answer in the positive. I have given such an appalling account of myself these past few days, I suppose I thought it was advisable to make sure of my route before proceeding.'

'Oh.' *Very well, Lilith, breathe again. You remember how it's done.*

'There is no need to break into a gallop when you can enjoy the journey at a sedate trot,' he went on, apparently warming to his theme.

'Yes,' she said judiciously, 'but not, perhaps, so slowly that one falls asleep and misses the scenery.'

He laughed aloud. 'I will keep that in mind. Bear with me, Lilith. Not being in control of my life is not what I am used to.'

Nor me, Edward. Nor me.

★   ★   ★

Well done, Ned. How to make a mull of a perfectly easy matter. And now there was the sound of gravel under the carriage wheels as they turned on to the Cheveley Park drive. He withdrew his hand reluctantly from hers.

'You will have noticed I am not very fluent when making speeches,' he said by way of oblique apology.

Her lips twitched. 'That's going to make your presentation after dinner next Wednesday awkward.'

'I shall treat it as a lecture,' he said bravely. 'I have it on good authority that I am that rare thing, an enthusiastic speaker.'

Her lips were definitely trembling now. 'How fortunate.'

The door was opened and the night air rushed in. The Cheveley footman handed them out.

'Into the fray,' murmured Ned.

And abruptly, all trace of laughter was wiped from her face. She took a deep breath. 'Indeed.'

By Cheveley standards, the party at dinner was not large, but as the daughter of the fourth Lord Fitzgilbert and the sister of the fifth, Lilith was placed too far up the table for him (a lowly commoner, even if his brother did own a reasonable portion of Hampshire and an even bigger chunk of Scotland) to talk to. Instead he found himself being polite to a colonial bigwig's outspoken wife on one side and fending off the gushing admiration of the bigwig's daughter on the other. It was with relief that he saw the duchess rise at the end of the meal and signal the withdrawal of the ladies. Lilith, as he had speedily realised from the few glimpses he'd had of her conversing intelligently during the meal, was well used to these sort of events. Too much so to even glance his way as she passed.

A hale, vigorous gentleman with the sheen of good living to him plumped down next to Ned. 'My thanks for entertaining m'wife and daughter,' said this gentleman, sticking out a hand. 'Sir John Highside. I'm an East Indies merchant.'

Highside . . . Highside . . . Why did he know the name? It had been teasing him throughout the meal. 'Not at all,' he said civilly. 'Your wife is a fund of knowledge on a part of the world I have never visited. A most interesting conversationalist.' *Highside! Of course. He had provided one of Kerr's references.* 'I think you once employed a Donald Kerr, didn't you?'

'Kerr? No, can't say I remember the name.'

'Oh, perhaps I have the wrong man. Scottish, stocky, very efficient.'

'Never employed a Scot in my life. Can't make out the accent. What did you think of m'daughter, eh? Pretty little puss, ain't she?'

With alarm, Ned saw where this dialogue might be leading. 'A veritable English rose,' he lied. 'If my own affections were not already engaged, her no doubt numerous suitors would have found their ranks swelled before we had reached the second remove.'

This answer pleased the nabob so greatly that he launched into a rambling anecdote of a young sprig of fashion who had fallen so importunately in love with his daughter that he'd had to take a shotgun to him.

Ned smiled and sympathised and wondered for the next twenty minutes if Kerr had ever told him the truth about anything.

★ ★ ★

'Kerr gave a false reference?' said Lilith. They were sitting on one of the most uncomfortable sofas she had ever encountered. She had nearly slid off it twice and now understood why it had been the only one vacant in the long room.

'Yes, but I don't understand it. He is a good secretary. Why would he need to invent a reference?'

'Presumably because he was also a thief.'

'I daresay. I am becoming increasingly angry about having been taken in by him. Have you had a pleasant evening?'

She gave a tiny shrug. 'It was much like any dinner in town. The conversation was unexceptional, if not stimulating.'

It was not the dinner that had been the problem, it was resolutely not looking down the table during the meal to see who Edward was being entertained by and then avoiding the duchess's probing questions afterwards. 'I found myself mostly thinking of your dinner and what Catherine and I will need to do to prepare for it. At least yours is gentlemen only, so I do not have the added challenge of separating husbands and wives and keeping the amorously-inclined away from the innocents.'

'More things I have never realised were necessary. I see why you said you were looking forward to a break from all that. Would you miss it if you were to make a prolonged stay in the country?'

Was this him cautiously advancing to the next step? Lilith answered honestly. 'I have run Bedford Square since Mama died. It never occurred to any of us that I would not, even though I was then only seventeen. When Papa remarried — to a very silly woman — I organised her soirées because I didn't want him to be made ridiculous. After he passed away I continued to organise them to save Benedict from embarrassment. I act as his hostess on formal occasions for much the same reason. Now I wish to be selfish. I said to Ben before I came here that if I'd been male I would be tucked up in one of the universities by now and would likely never leave the library.'

'Looking at you tonight, that would be a shame.'

His eyes were warm and caused no little agitation in Lilith's breast. 'There,' she said, charmed, 'and I thought you claimed to have no social graces.'

He grinned. 'Is it not possible to study *and* order a household? You said your mother wrote.'

'Pamphlets on social reform and how expression in the arts enlarges the mind. She could only do so because Papa encouraged it. He was very proud of her. She ran the house too, but with a light hand.'

'Ladies are humbling,' said Edward

glumly. 'When I submerse myself in work, I find whole days or weeks go by. I resent the time taken to make all the petty decisions of day-to-day life.'

Lilith hid a smile. 'I had noticed.'

'But no more. I am a changed man — or I am endeavouring to be. Lilith, do you think you might look favourably on a man who . . . what is the matter?'

Lilith was staring across the room in horror. 'Edward, may we vacate this horribly slippery couch and walk about the room for a bit?'

He stood immediately. 'Certainly. Who are we avoiding?'

'Sir Mortimer Vale,' she said. She laid her hand lightly on his arm, drawing an entirely non-cerebral comfort from the capable muscles concealed beneath the fine material of his coat. 'Do you know him?'

'Can't say I do.' His gaze swept the room lazily. 'Unless he's the florid gentleman who smells disgustingly of violets.'

'That's exactly who he is. I can't

imagine what he is doing here and I . . . have a particular reason for not speaking to him. Would you mind very much if I suddenly contracted a headache?'

'Nothing would please me more,' answered Edward promptly. 'It has often piqued me that gentlemen cannot do the same. Let us go and take our leave of her Grace.'

The Duchess of Rutland had a decided gleam in her eye as Lilith made her excuses. 'Call on me,' she breathed in her ear, in a way that left very little room for prevarication.

'As soon as I have anything worth telling,' Lilith replied, sotto voce. 'By the by, I am surprised to see Sir Mortimer Vale present. I thought he rarely left London.'

The duchess made a moue of distaste. 'Wretched man. Sally Jersey cultivates him for the gossip, but I never trust these scented ones. Unfortunately I could do little else but extend an invitation when Lady Wellham told me he was visiting. I imagine there is a reason he is not in town, but I have no desire to hear what it is.'

There was a small delay whilst Edward's carriage was called. To Lilith's annoyance, Sir Mortimer Vale chose this moment to saunter into the entrance hall.

'Miss Fitzgilbert, I thought I recognised you across the room. An unexpected pleasure to find you so far from your normal haunts,' he said. 'Might I say how charmingly feminine you look this evening.'

Lilith inclined her head. 'Sir Mortimer.'

Had she thought Edward could not act a part? Quality personified, he took Lilith's shawl from a waiting footman and said, 'I am afraid Miss Fitzgilbert is unwell. Do not let us keep you from the company.'

Sir Mortimer's gaze took in Edward's broad shoulders and splendid physique. His nostrils flared with undisguised interest. 'I beg your pardon,' he said silkily. 'Do accept my wishes for a speedy recovery, Miss Fitzgilbert.'

They watched him stroll away. Lilith could not repress a shudder.

'That gentleman,' remarked Edward, as he draped the wrap around her with savage possessiveness, 'had better keep his proclivities from being quite so much on show if he doesn't want to attract the wrong sort of attention.'

She glanced up at him. 'Is it so obvious then? How can you tell?'

He seemed to realise he was crushing the fringe of her shawl and smoothed it out with repentant fingers. 'I have travelled about the world a good deal,' he said gravely.

'As have I. Evidently not to the same places. All the same, I wish he were not in Newmarket.'

'I have rarely taken a more instant dislike to anyone. I do not generally advocate violence, but if you would like me to run him out of town, I will ask Rutland the best way of going about it.'

'Thus embroiling yourself in a

scandal and ensuring no one invests in your Hellenic excavation. I doubt such a sacrifice is necessary.' She paused. 'You do not ask me why?'

He smiled down at her. 'Why would I? I am very pleased with whatever brought you to Newmarket.'

'You did not think so at first.'

'As I am sure your mother would have remarked, it is the sign of a flexible mind to admit one's mistakes.'

17

On Saturday, Lilith arrived at Ditton Place to the unwelcome news that Kerr had insisted on getting up and partaking of breakfast.

'Were you civil?' she asked curiously when Edward joined her in the library.

'I adopted a perfectly pleasant tone, said I had managed well enough and I would give him our new records when we were certain he was strong enough to take up his duties again. I'm not sure I have ever seen him look more annoyed.'

'I hope we replaced everything correctly so he doesn't suspect you are aware of his deception.'

Edward waved that away. 'The doctor has warned him his memory may be faulty. Besides, any breakfast of Mrs Bell's devising will very soon send him back to his bed.' He sat down beside her. 'What have you found to read this morning?'

'I am playing truant with an old sketchbook of yours. Your draughtsmanship is very good. Where is this? It is beautiful.'

She turned to the page that had fascinated her. It was a drawing of stone columns built into the side of a cliff, with graceful pedestals and statues set between the arches.

Edward stilled. His hand briefly touched the page. 'Caunus,' he said, a curious sadness in his voice.

Lilith turned to look at him. 'What's the matter?'

'I'd forgotten this, or rather, I'd pushed it to the back of my mind. Caunus was a city in ancient Persia. It had been ruled by both the Greeks and the Romans until the area was overrun by the Turks some four hundred years ago. It is all ruins now. I was with a team doing some explorations. The foreman had a daughter — a child really — who drew like an angel. This is not my sketch, it is hers. She was always withdrawn except when she had a pencil in her hand. I used to ask her to sketch fragments simply to see the change in her. It wasn't until later I realised the problem. She was addicted to opium, even so young. A great many of the Turks are. One night she took so much she danced off the side of the cliff.' He looked at Lilith. 'As you know, it makes those who use it happy, and when it wears off they are wretched and ill, so they take more. People in this country recognise only the benefits.' He continued to leaf through the sketches, his expression remote.

His sorrow touched an answering chord in Lilith. 'She has left something of herself behind in her drawings,' she said. 'Her memory is preserved. Perhaps if she had been older, that is all she would have wished.' She took a quick breath. 'Francesco — our artist who died — painted with fire and light. He did not regret what he was doing. I never knew his talent before he was addicted, so I cannot judge the difference it made. I have two of his paintings at home. A reminder of him, but also a reminder that in forcing talent, we destroy it.' She fell silent. 'I am sermonising. I apologise.'

'Don't be sorry. I enjoy talking to you on serious matters as well as lighter subjects. It's a strange thing, looking at these drawings again has made me realise I was more involved with the native workmen in those days. Perhaps it was because I was not in charge of the exploration, but I talked to them and got to know them a little. I have not done that in recent years.'

'Because you have had your secretary with you to act as an intermediary so you could concentrate on the work?'

He nodded. 'I believe so, yes, but if I *had* talked to the Egyptian porters, I would have been aware of the poverty. It is a mistake to allow oneself to be cocooned from the everyday.'

'A mistake you will not make again, I think. Was Ricky with you in Caunus?'

'Yes, he was only a schoolboy but I wasn't going to leave him with my father for the summer. It was his first time out of England, so he was dazzled by all the new experiences. I don't know whether he even realised half the workers were addicted to opium. Certainly I can never take him back there, it would be too easy to lapse.'

And even if the greatest antiquarian discoveries of the age were to be made there, Edward would bypass them, would give up his own chance at glory, in order to keep his brother safe. Lilith impulsively covered his hand with hers. 'I do not think you need to worry. Ricky's writing is strong enough not to need the stimulus, providing people keep telling him so. Artists, in my experience, require constant praise and encouragement. It is unfortunate that no one has yet appreciated the accrued benefit of hard work.'

'I daresay it is too prosaic for them.'

'Indeed. I used to encourage my

stepmother's protégés by comparing an artistic creation to the building of a house. You only have to observe the progress of Mr Nash's new terraces to realise there are months of confusion and dust and noise, then suddenly the project is properly house-shaped, pleasing to behold and functional.'

Edward grinned. 'That is a good parallel. Why do you not use it now?'

She glanced at him ruefully. 'I realised that whatever a house looks like, whatever its shortcomings, there will always be people glad to live in it. Nobody will buy a bad painting. A bad epic poem remains bad.'

He laughed. 'You are a realist.'

There was a cough from the doorway. Kerr stood there, shock on his face, smoothed away in an instant.

Lilith quickly withdrew her hand, conscious that she was sitting rather close to Edward, even though Hester was sewing in the corner to provide respectability.

'You should be resting,' said Edward,

looking up calmly. 'I am not expecting you to work today. We have sufficient staff to see to the running of the house, so there is no need for you to do anything except recover your health. We were lucky that Miss Fitzgilbert is accustomed to running a large household. In your absence, she knew just who we would need.'

Lilith gave a depreciative smile. 'It was not so difficult. The list of servants left by your former housekeeper was most useful. After the majority had been re-hired, it was simply a case of replacing those who had found new positions.'

Kerr's expression became even more wooden. 'If I could perhaps review the list?'

'Certainly,' said Lilith. 'I will write you out a fair copy this afternoon.'

'That will be all, Kerr,' said Edward. 'If you wish for some fresh air, the gardeners have already made the ground a lot more secure to walk on.'

The secretary hovered a moment

longer, then left. Edward looked at Lilith. 'I hope your brother finds something on him soon. I am not sure for how much longer I can bear to have him in my house.'

Lilith reached for her reticule. 'I'd forgotten! A letter came from Benedict. I should have mentioned it straight away. His agent located Kerr's mother from the name and address we sent. Her second husband is an apothecary in Dundee. The agent fell into conversation with this Mr Fraser. This is the interesting part. His previous assistant was his wife's son by her first marriage. Mr Fraser took him on as an apprentice and trained him up, but he now has a post in London!'

Edward stared. 'Kerr used to be an apothecary? Why would he change careers? I suppose it explains the false references if mine was the first secretarial post he had applied for.'

'It would also explain why his medicine cabinet looked so professional,' said Lilith. 'It was evidently his own, from when he was practising. Oh . . . '

'What is it? What else have you thought of?'

'Kerr's chest was full of medicines,' she said slowly. 'Including many, many packets of opium tablets. Hester commented on them. Why would he need so much?'

'Ready for the next expedition, perhaps. Whatever else he is, I'll swear Kerr is not an opium eater. He has never betrayed the slightest symptom. If he was, his stupor when we dosed him would make no sense.'

'No, that's true. There can be nothing in it. It just seemed strange that he would have such a quantity.' She turned back to Edward's sketchbook. 'Where are these other places?'

As he told her about them, painting tiny word pictures of the places, an idea coalesced in Lilith's head. She tried to push it away, but it persisted. Kerr couldn't have been so wicked, surely?

'I was thinking,' she said, feeling nausea rise up in her throat, 'when

Francesco came to us, he was already addicted. I remember him often clutching his stomach and gasping that he must have relief. Our housekeeper gave him a little laudanum in some wine, as we are accustomed to take for digestive problems. He laughed bitterly and said he was far beyond that. He wrest the bottle from her and drank it down as if it was small beer. It was she who told me how it can take you and not let go, how people need more and more, in ever-greater concentration.'

'I am sorry for him, but what are you saying?'

'I just wonder, if we compared Ricky's bottle with the one in Mrs Gunn's chest, whether they would taste the same. And if they don't, then we should ask Ricky where his came from.'

'You think Ricky's may be a different strength? Do you have the key to Mrs Gunn's chest?'

'She left her ring of keys in the drawer in her room.'

Edward got to his feet. 'Then I will

ask Ferris for Ricky's bottle and meet you there.'

Within a few minutes, she, Edward, Ferris and Hester were all in the housekeeper's room. The household medicine chest was indeed handsome, with doors on both front and back and several deep drawers. Lilith unstoppered the bottle of laudanum and upended it to get a drop on her finger.

'Wait,' said Edward, catching her wrist before she could touch it to her tongue. 'Why is this for you to do?'

She glanced at him in surprise. 'If it makes me sleepy, I can be more easily spared than you. Definitely laudanum,' she said, making a face. She did the same with Ricky's bottle and immediately scrubbed her mouth with her handkerchief. 'Ugh. So bitter. I am not surprised it laid Kerr out. This is very strong indeed.' A troubled expression crossed her face. 'Ricky cannot realise just how strong or he would have warned us.' *Which meant her terrible suspicion had been right.*

Lilith had tried both medicines without even considering asking someone else to do it. Ned was so stunned that it was a moment before her words sank in. 'Strong? Then the apothecary where he purchased it should be prosecuted. There is no shop label on the bottle. Do you know where it came from, Ferris?'

The valet shook his head. 'You'll need to speak to Mr Richard about that.'

Lilith stoppered the bottle soberly and passed it to Ferris. 'Edward, when Ricky fetched this, Kerr looked at it in utter horror.'

Sickness churned his stomach as he realised what she was saying. 'And Donald Kerr trained as an apothecary *and* he is oversupplied with opium tablets!' Rage slammed into him. 'By God, if he is responsible for Ricky's dependence on that filthy stuff, I will rend him limb from limb.'

'Not until he has led my brother to

Flint.' Lilith took his balled fist and uncurled his fingers. 'And I think, perhaps hold yourself in check when you ask Ricky where he got the bottle?'

He looked down at her bent head. He was still strung taut with anger, but the touch of her hand on his was calming. 'You are annoyingly wise,' he said. 'No doubt I should be grateful.'

She uncurled his other hand. 'No, I am as furious as you. Kerr is vile and wicked, but I would not have you waste your life on him.'

She cared. And there was too much wrath in him to appreciate her. Everything was knotted and snarled together. Damn Kerr. Damn him to eternity.

Ferris coughed. 'I'll lock this away, sir. Miss Hepple, I wonder if you might have a few moments to advise me on a tear in Mr Richard's best coat?'

With his valet's diplomatic words, the world righted itself. Knots and snarls there may be, but Ferris was in no doubt as to what should be of prime importance in his master's life. 'We are embarrassing them,' said Ned. His voice sounded husky to his own ears. He reversed their hands so he was now holding both of Lilith's.

She raised her face to his, open and amused, and also a little shy. 'Do you think so? I was taking their withdrawal as approval.'

'Lilith, we have known each other a very short while, and circumstances keep intruding on us. This is not the ideal time, and I am not at all sure I am the right man to give you the future you deserve, but may I ask your brother if I might pay my addresses to you?'

'Well, you *can*,' she replied candidly, 'but I would very much prefer that you asked me first.'

He was unprepared for the rush of happiness that swept through him. He tightened his grip on her hands, bent his head and . . .

And then a sound at the door had them springing apart like rabbits at the first pull of the gamekeeper's shotgun.

'This room will do very well, I think,' Lilith said from over by the table. 'It only needs a light dust and the fire lit to take the chill off it a couple of days before Mrs Smith arrives.'

'I will tell Peter to see to it,' replied Ned in the same cool tone. He realised she was shielding the medicine cabinet still on the table and strolled in that direction. 'Your fund of household knowledge has been invaluable. I am very grateful. Is there anything else you think we . . . Yes, Kerr, did you want me? What is it?'

'I . . . ' His secretary darted a suspicious look between them. 'I wondered if you had given any thought to the speech for your dinner and whether you wished me to take it down for you.'

It was so obviously an invented errand that hatred of the man swamped Ned. How dare his machinations taint Ned's new, breathtaking feelings for Lilith? 'Not at this moment,' he snapped. 'But you have reminded me

— why are we holding the dinner here and not in London as I asked?'

Kerr's air of faint surprise was masterly. 'I beg your pardon. I must have misunderstood you. I fear it is too late to change it now.'

'Did you also misunderstand when I instructed you to secure the services of the town house chef for the occasion?'

'He does not travel into the country.'

'Which is why it was to be held in town! Did you genuinely imagine Mrs Bell would be an adequate substitute? To serve an important dinner to gentlemen of taste and discernment, accustomed to the finest of dining?'

'I had formed the intention of interviewing . . . '

'So much so that you have not even enquired about that, but instead come in here asking about my speech. Well, I have saved you the trouble. All is arranged. You may take yourself off for the remainder of the day and recover your strength.'

Kerr's pale face grew even more

pinched. 'Very good, sir.'

'Was that wise?' asked Lilith when he had gone. She quickly locked the medicine chest and dropped the ring of keys into her reticule.

Ned swung the chest back to the far wall. 'He has been with me long enough that if I had not ripped up at him, he would have found it even more suspicious than my taking the organisation on myself.' He gave a harsh laugh. 'I had forgotten what a poor prospect I am as a life partner. I believe I had best not approach Lord Fitzgilbert after all.' He held the door open for her to precede him back to the library.

He became aware of her studying him. 'I own I could wish your secretary had not come in just then,' she said. 'Circumstances do indeed keep intruding on us. But as you yourself said, we are on a journey. We have plenty of time. Meanwhile, there is not so much to do here that you cannot be spared to work at the site.'

'Except Ricky and the scholars have

formed the intention of walking the length of the dyke to Reach today.'

'Then we could join your friend Mr Thornley outside.'

'Thornley has taken advantage of their absence to drive himself into Bury St Edmunds. And before you suggest I go to the ditch by myself, I am too cross now to settle to the work and also I do not trust Kerr not to creep around here and make mischief.'

For answer, she chuckled and gestured to the footmen in the hall and the maids dusting the stair banister. 'Dodging between the staff, presumably. I am sure Woods can find you some silver to polish if you have need of occupation.'

'And have the servants up in arms at me for taking their work?'

'Then bend your mind to the problem of how we are to prevent Kerr meeting Catherine when she starts scrubbing out the kitchen the moment Mrs Bell leaves. I do not think Nicholas Dacre standing by the baize door brandishing a horsewhip will quite serve.'

He felt his anger abating at the absurd picture she painted. 'Kerr has given me the answer himself. I shall spend the day requesting him to write down ever more embellishments to my speech. I confess I was hoping your brother might have discovered sufficient about his link with Flint to render his continued presence here unnecessary by then. Lilith, do you really think Kerr was increasing the opium level in Ricky's laudanum without telling him?'

She gave an unhappy nod.

'It is all so fantastic. Theft I can understand, but Ricky is the most inoffensive soul in Christendom. Why would he do such a thing? Yes, Ferris?'

'I thought it might interest you to know Mr Kerr is suffering from stomach cramps, sir. It looks to me like the sort Mr Richard had earlier in the year, only he is calling it indigestion. He's shut himself in his room and says he'll doctor himself. Mr Woods suggested you and Miss Fitzgilbert might like coffee in the library.'

'Thank you,' answered Lilith. 'That sounds very pleasant. Shall we sit by the window, Edward? It seems a shame to squander the winter sunshine.'

Ned gave a reluctant smile. She was preserving the semblance of normality, giving them time to learn about each other. He scooped up a pile of Ricky's scattered pages from the window table to clear it. 'Ha,' he said, glancing at them. 'Evidently Ricky's rendition of Roman history to the children at Furze House has inspired him to rework one of his early epics. I remember this one quite well, but it must be several years old.'

'May I see?'

'Let me sort the verses into order. He has excelled himself writing on the backs of old pages here.' He passed her the first couple, reversed a sheet from a yellowing report, then . . . then took the sheet back and searched for the word in the report that had caught his eye. Good heavens . . .

'Edward?'

'Listen to this,' he said. '*Alexander Kerr, tacksman, to be relocated with his family to a five acre holding in the coastal area above Dundee . . .* '

'What does it mean?' she asked, sounding puzzled.

Ned gave a mirthless laugh. 'What was it you said the other day? Why does Kerr hate me? This could be the answer.' He took a pen from the stand and a fresh sheet of paper. 'I need to write to my brother's man of business.'

Lilith picked up the discarded page. 'I see the name, but I don't understand.'

'Has your family has never held land in Scotland? This is a part of a clearance report. Some fifteen years ago, my father decided the Scottish estates would provide him with more income if he cleared them of tenants and put the land to sheep instead. I thought his actions iniquitous and unnecessary and said so, and was bawled out for my pains. Kerr's family might have been amongst the dispossessed. A tacksman is the equivalent of a squire here, with status and a good house, responsibility and land to sublet. To go from that to farming a five-acre croft would be sufficient and more to cause a son or nephew of the house to hate the landowner, don't you think?'

'Indeed I do! I hesitate to speak ill of your progenitors, Edward, but such an act is callous in the extreme. Kerr might be motivated by revenge then? He makes you and Ricky suffer because he was made to suffer by your family?'

'It would answer the case very well. I am asking Henry's man to check what family this Alexander Kerr had. I will also send a note to your brother. It becomes clearer, Lilith, but I do not think we have the whole yet. Why does Kerr have that list of house-party names, for example? And what was the original hold Flint had on him?'

Lilith looked out of the window. Her gaze was troubled. 'Edward, this is such a lovely house. I do not like to think of it containing Mr Kerr's hatred. Is that fanciful?'

'Not at all. When we have solved this and put him safely in charge, we will open all the casements and let a cleansing wind blow through it.' *And perhaps we can talk, properly talk.*

He finished writing his letters while Lilith sat next to him, sipping her coffee and reading Ricky's poem. It felt very right, her being there. He *would* say something more, he determined, as soon as they had walked down to the stables and given Chilcott the letters to take into Newmarket.

But as they strolled through the wintry sunshine, she said, 'I've remembered something from last week. Catherine's brother and sister-in-law visited her after church. Mrs Bowman was full of a Mr Fraser, a Scottish gentleman who was passing through Kennet End and who was most interested in her household.'

He gave a sharp intake of breath. 'Kerr. It had to be. Finding out if

Catherine was living there.' He glared at the upper windows of the house where Kerr's rooms lay. 'What did she tell him?'

'Nothing to his purpose, though that was more luck than anything else. It seems the Bowmans rarely acknowledge Catherine if they don't have to. She was involved in a scandal, you see, and as this Mr Fraser had opened the conversation with how distinguished Mrs Bowman looked, she would certainly not bring in anything so detrimental to her standing.'

'Then we may scrape by.' He heaved an irritated sigh. 'I shall have to insist Kerr comes to the village church here with Ricky and me tomorrow to prevent him trying again. He will glower in silent disapproval of the rector's taste for forgiveness and brotherly love, but it will no doubt be much to the benefit of my immortal soul.' He paused. 'And the rest of the day I should really spend with the scholars. How do you pass your Sundays?'

She smiled up at him. 'Tomorrow, Catherine and I will go to church and then put our heads to devising a menu for the dinner.'

'Now I feel guilty. You should be reading or drawing, not slaving over the very same chores you came into the country to have a break from.'

An enchanting blush stained her cheeks. 'Nonsense. It is something I can do and there is pride afterwards when all goes well. I only hope Kerr's hatred of you does not prompt him to ruin it. I did suggest to Benedict that he should come down, but he said in his letter he is engaged all next week.'

'That is a shame. I have a pressing need to speak to your brother — and *not* about my secretary. Lilith, I . . . '

But there was a boisterous shout as Ricky and the scholars came into view. 'Ned! Ned, we've had the most famous walk. You should have come. It was glorious.'

Ned let out a frustrated growl. One day he might be allowed to talk to Lilith beyond the point when things were starting to get interesting.

18

It was evident to Lilith on Monday morning that Edward was labouring under a strong sense of ill usage.

'Why am I going to the wine merchants in Bury St Edmunds when I would prefer to be here?' he said, standing on the drive with his hat in his hand and the wind ruffling his hair.

'In order to give an impressive dinner, secure funding for your expedition and not be a laughing stock. Here are the extra ingredients Catherine would like. You do not have to understand them, simply hand each portion to the shops she has indicated.'

Edward ran his eye over the lists. 'You are making me hungry. This will be a handsome dinner indeed. Suppose I am reconsidering the Greece trip?'

Warmth gathered in her chest. 'Why would you do that?'

'I might have an entirely different notion of how to spend the summer.'

The warmth spread until it was heating her face. *What sort of notion?*

Behind Edward, Chilcott held the horses' heads with benign patience. Donald Kerr sat inside the carriage, watching them stonily through the window. It was not a pleasant scrutiny. 'Then you can bank the subscriptions for next year instead,' she said. 'Go. Say goodbye to your scholars and your friend and get your secretary out of our way. We are going to be very busy.'

'I have said goodbye to them, and Thornley has already gone. He has an assignation at the opera tonight.'

'That's fortunate. Molly is coming with Catherine to help scrub. Having bid him a profitable farewell last night, it could be a trifle awkward to encounter him in broad daylight whilst wrapped in a skivvy's apron.'

Edward looked amused. 'You don't know Thornley. Also, I am persuaded

332

you should have no awareness of such transactions.'

'Furze House is a very enlightening environment. Away with you. The carriage is blocking the drive and Mr Grimes cannot get past. The sooner he takes the scholars, the sooner he can return for Mrs Bell. I promise you will not know the place once she has gone.'

Edward captured her hand and raised it to his lips, bending his head so his errant lock of hair fell forward. 'You have the most beautiful eyes, Lilith. Are you aware how much I am looking forward to Thursday when this madness is over?'

The pool of warmth in Lilith's chest threatened to overwhelm her. 'I was thinking,' she said, striving for an even tone, 'that until Thursday we should be ... we should be simply friends. Associates working together ... '

Breathe, Lilith, you are making a fool of yourself

'The rate at which we are constantly interrupted,' he remarked dryly, 'there seems little chance of anything else.'

He tipped his hat to her and strode off. That should have been her cue to go inside and start work. Instead, her gaze lingered on the carriage as it bore him away. Beautiful eyes indeed. Did he not know he could make a whole roomful of society women feel weak just by looking at him?

The scholars were the next to leave. 'I shall miss them,' said Ricky as they waved them off. He glanced at Lilith shyly. 'I am determined to ask Ned about entering Cambridge. I wanted to this year, but Kerr said we couldn't afford it and that I shouldn't tease Ned because it would make him ashamed when he had to refuse.'

'Mr Kerr is remarkably busy about your brother's business,' replied Lilith tartly. 'However, as we now know he was taking money out of the accounts for his own purposes, I should not let the finances worry you. In any case, your older brother could surely be applied to for a contribution.'

'I hadn't thought of Henry. I have been . . . a bit muddled this year.'

And Kerr no doubt contrived to keep you that way. Lilith made a quick decision. 'Ricky, I have no right to ask, but was it Donald Kerr who supplied you with the laudanum?'

He looked unhappy. 'I promised I would not say.'

'It was not the action of a friend,' she said gently.

'You don't think he might simply have been mistaken? He dosed me with it first for a stomach complaint, then noticed it was improving my writing. He said it had been demonstrated by many great poets that simple living, combined with regular draughts of laudanum, was the key to unlocking talent.'

At that moment, Lilith was quite sorry Edward had taken Kerr to Bury St Edmunds. She had a fierce desire to bundle the man's belongings together and ship him somewhere savage and remote by the earliest tide. 'Ricky, I cannot believe he was unaware of how much the drug takes as well as gives. I have had a great deal to do with artists. It *can* help the muse, but I find the best writers are those with open, enquiring minds — people who live in the world and mix with many different people. Entering one of the universities will do you far more good than anything out of a bottle, and you can still soak up the history you love by accompanying your brother on his summer expeditions.'

'Then I will ask Ned. It's all right, Lilith, I don't like Kerr nearly as much as I did.'

'Good. Report to Woods and see what he has for you to do. We are all of us on menial duties today.'

Ricky brightened up. 'Will he let me beat the rugs? I love whacking them and seeing the dust motes fly away into the air. Poor Ned, missing this.'

★　★　★

'I do not see,' said Kerr stiffly, 'how accompanying you to Bury St Edmunds is the most effective use of my time. There are many other items regarding the dinner that need addressing.'

'But no need for you to do them,' replied Ned blandly. 'Miss Fitzgilbert has organised scores of similar occasions in town. Having accepted her offer to see to the whole, I cannot now insult her by dividing the tasks.'

Kerr's lips pursed. 'Very obliging of Miss Fitzgilbert. I hope her altruism does not have another goal. I would be derelict in my duty if I did not warn that your present finances are insufficient to allow any changes to your establishment.'

Rage burned in Ned's breast at Kerr's insolence. 'For that you are partly responsible,' he said curtly. 'If you had not employed a rogue as a butler, Atkins would not have robbed me of half-a-year's wages. We will use the journey time to work on my speech.'

'I hardly think words taken down over fifteen miles of country road are likely to be legible.' It was as near to a snap as Ned had ever heard from his secretary.

'Invaluable for organising my thoughts, however. You can make a fair copy when we are back.'

Once in Bury St Edmunds, he spun out the tasks for as long as he was able, getting an unpraiseworthy frisson of satisfaction every time he discovered a new establishment that they needed to visit. Returning to the Angel Hotel from the final one, Ned halted outside *Wm Taylor — Goldsmith*, his eye drawn by an item in the window that he'd noticed earlier that day.

'What does Miss Fitzgilbert require from here?' asked Kerr acidly. 'Gold leaf to embellish the quails?'

'A pretty thought,' said Ned, 'but I had something else in mind.'

The goldsmith himself, a cheerful, rounded man, came forward. 'The peridot necklace, sir? A fine choice. A fine choice indeed.' He bustled to the window and brought it forth. 'It will be for a special lady, I daresay.'

'Very special,' said Ned absently. It was beautiful. As elegant as Lilith herself, the stones matching the colour of her eyes under a cloudless sky. He envisioned himself fastening it around her neck, pictured her lips, parted with delight . . .

'If you wish,' said the goldsmith, 'I could arrange bracelets and earrings to match.'

'Just the necklace,' said Ned, curbing his wayward imagination. 'I can always add to the set if it finds favour.'

'Indeed you can, sir,' agreed Mr Taylor.

'Sir,' said Kerr in a choked voice behind him, 'you cannot . . . '

'Cannot what?' asked Ned, swinging around and fixing his secretary with a frigid eye. 'Cannot have this valuable piece delivered to the Angel along with the spices and the sack of oranges and the crates of wine and port? Indeed not. I will take it with me.'

If Kerr looked as if he had swallowed a wasp, it was nothing to his expression on alighting from the carriage at Ditton Place to discover that a new cook and footman had arrived from the Fitzgilbert town house and that Lilith Fitzgilbert and her maid had established themselves in Ned's late mother's suite until Thursday, the better to oversee the dinner preparations.

Ned sauntered into the house, comfortable in the certainty of a day very well spent indeed.

       ★   ★   ★

'Mary is well satisfied with her new domain, and Joshua is delighted to find himself second only to Woods in the hierarchy,' reported Lilith to Edward as they walked in the grounds the following day. She had a trug over one arm, unearthed for her by an ancient gardener. The man himself followed a little way behind, keeping up an occasionally audible monologue about what might have been available to decorate the house had he not been turned off six months before.

'Breakfast this morning was particularly agreeable,' said Edward. 'Both the food and the company.'

He was enjoying this altogether too much. 'Your secretary did not think so,' she replied, some of the pleasure leaving her at the memory. 'Every time I glanced his way he was looking daggers drawn at me.'

'Chrysanthemums,' mourned the gardener. 'Lovely bed there used to be. Wouldn't hardly think it now.'

'Ignore Kerr. He has forgotten what it is like to eat good food. Lilith . . . '

'As for that there laurel hedge, just look at the way it's grown over the pathway. Fair makes a body weep to see it.'

'Laurel,' said Lilith, pausing to assess the offending glossy foliage. 'Sixsmith, if you trim the hedges back, I can use the cut branches in some of those great pottery urns Mr Edward collected on his travels.'

The would-be suitor was abruptly replaced by the antiquarian. 'Lilith, those urns are ancient artefacts.'

She beamed at him. 'So appropriate, don't you think? You needn't worry, I will not add water or earth to them, just the branches. And perhaps some of the ivy Sixsmith was complaining about that is choking the fruit trees in his orchard. It will look very striking, trailing over the sides of the pots.'

The old gardener eyed her with rheumy approval. 'I'll need to get my grandson over if there's to be any swarming up of trees.'

'Splendid. He'll enjoy that. Now then, which other green shrubs need pruning? We will dazzle Mr Edward's potential investors with our brilliance.'

'They will not be the only ones dazzled,' said Edward. 'I swear you have got my whole household eating out of your hand.'

'Apart from Kerr,' said Lilith. 'That colourless politeness is worse than a sword thrust. He dislikes me very much, Edward.'

'The devil take him. I will not have you made uncomfortable. I will keep him busy and out of your way. On Thursday you will be back at Furze House, then as soon as Henry returns to Hampshire, I shall remove to town and your brother can set a watch on Kerr. Pray heaven it will not be too long before his agents find what they are looking for.'

★ ★ ★

By Wednesday, the change in Ditton Place was extraordinary. Surfaces gleamed, walls were dust free, curtains had been shaken and re-hung. Lilith's arrangements of winter evergreens enhanced every architectural feature.

Catherine had slipped quietly into the back premises as she had the past two days, and her assistant from Furze House was also lending a hand with the preparations. Rich scents of cooking wafted enticingly whenever a door was left ajar.

The only sour note was the continued presence of Donald Kerr.

'Nothing,' said Nicholas Dacre in frustration as he paced the housekeeper's room with Lilith and Edward. 'Yes, he is Alexander Kerr's son. Yes, the family was relocated to Dundee by your father's agent. That's where Mr Kerr senior died and Mrs Kerr subsequently married the apothecary Mr Fraser. Yes, the young Donald Kerr was taken on by Fraser as an apprentice. Once he qualified, he moved down to London and obtained a position at Harbottles until three years ago when he changed career to become your secretary. And that is all we know. The sketch Lilith made of him has been shown discreetly around Flint's known businesses, but he has such an unremarkable face that only the meat pie vendor in Wardour Street is prepared to swear he has seen him visiting the house. We will be reduced to intercepting every letter he writes and following him every minute of the day once you are back in town.'

Edward shrugged. 'Kerr will presumably report his failure in short order, so you may get a pointer to Flint sooner than you think. I hope so. I do not want him in my employ a moment beyond what is necessary. When I think of all he has done to damage Ricky and wreck this blasted dinner, I am amazed I have not already thrown him out.'

'It will be a very nice dinner,' corrected Lilith. 'Just keep Kerr away from the kitchen until Catherine and Nicholas have safely departed. I will be in here for the duration, ready to block the door if necessary. Woods knows to head him off, but it is more important for him to attend to your guests.'

Edward sighed. 'I feel another addition to my speech coming on. How Kerr has not yet murdered me for the number of times I have made him rewrite it, I do not know. I give you fair warning, Dacre. Not a moment longer than necessary.'

He headed back towards the library.

Nicholas returned to the kitchen. Lilith recounted the china and silver. She and Catherine had decided on two full courses, of nine dishes and seven, removing fish with a white soup at the beginning of the first course, and featuring a cold jugged hare, sent down from Bedford Square with the new cook, as a prime component of the second course.

The activity in the domestic offices, coupled with the delicious smells, drew the attention of everyone in the house. Lilith lost count of the number of times she chased Ricky back to the main house and even Edward strolled down to the housekeeper's room on the pretext of reminding her how fond the Duke of Rutland was of orange syllabub. Nicholas sharpened knives slowly in a corner of the kitchen, remaining watchful the whole time.

Lilith didn't object to any of the visitors except Kerr, who was assiduous in enquiring in a dispassionate tone if there was anything he could do.

'Thank you, no,' she repeated for at least the fourth time, standing squarely across the passage. 'Though I believe Woods would appreciate a list of the guests so he can keep count of how many more arrivals are expected during the course of the evening.'

They were interrupted by two footmen, come to set up trestle tables along the passage for the dishes to be laid on before being taken to the dining room.

Lilith took one look and, 'I can't use these! Back outside to the barn where you found them and brush them down. Not a cobweb or spider do I want to see and neither will their various lordships. If you bring anything else indoors in the same state you may tell Cook you will be eating your own meal amongst the earwigs and beetles in the yard.'

The footmen grinned at this fine joke and reversed direction. When Lilith turned back, Kerr was gone.

Eventually, order restored, Lilith changed into a fresh plain gown, borrowed one of Catherine's lace caps and tied a housekeeper's apron around herself in case any of the guests should catch sight of her. She gave herself a sharp talking to. She had organised countless dinners, first for her father and then for her brother. Why her insides should be fluttering so badly today she had no idea.

Edward appeared in the passage, looking as distinguished as Ferris could make him. At the magnificent sight, Lilith's knees threatened to turn to water. Lord, he should warn a person when he was about to do that.

'I wanted to say thank you before everyone arrives.' He opened his hand to disclose a narrow box.

A present. He had given her a present. For the first time in Lilith's life, she had no idea how to respond. Several dozen thoughts chased through her mind, all expiring before they reached her tongue. 'There . . . there was no . . . ' She fumbled with the catch and lifted the lid. And gasped with pleasure at the peridot-set, silver filigree necklace nestling on cream satin.

Before she knew what he was about, he was fastening it around her neck. 'I saw it in Bury St Edmunds on Monday. Kerr was so tight-lipped about the expense I thought he was getting lockjaw. I was going to wait until tomorrow when I have something of a very particular nature to ask you, but . . . '

The baize door opened. Kerr stood there, silhouetted against the light. A draft made his shadow appear to stretch menacingly down the wall.

Edward ground his teeth. 'We'll talk later,' he said. Then he was striding back to the hall.

Lilith put a shaky hand to the necklace. Her insides were fluttering more than ever, but now for an entirely different reason.

★　★　★

The serving tables filled up and emptied as Woods and his entourage bore the dishes to the dining room. Lilith had drawn out a plan of where each was to go on the long table and made sure the younger footmen checked it before setting off. Two unplanned guests had arrived, but Catherine had allowed sufficient extra for that not to be noticed. The empty plates from the first remove came back along with a batch of compliments to the cook.

'Thank goodness for that,' muttered Lilith to Hester. 'Pass the praise on, would you?'

Hester went into the kitchen, reappearing shortly with a large glass bowl of orange syllabub. 'Mrs Redding says these might as well come out here to wait. This is the first one. Have you got the crystallised flowers to scatter on the top?'

'They're in the storeroom. I'll get them while you fetch the second bowl.'

She crossed the passage and had turned the storeroom handle when the baize door banged and the youngest footman pelted past her. To Lilith's horror she smelled violets and heard Woods say, 'Now then, sir, these are the back premises. You don't want to be in this part of the house.'

Sir Mortimer! He hadn't been on the guest list. He mustn't find her lurking here dressed as a housekeeper. The scandal would be immense! Lilith whisked into the storeroom and closed the door until only a crack remained open. There was a scuffle and a bluff protest from the passage, but to her relief she heard Woods firmly ushering Sir Mortimer back to the hall. She took a calming breath, then a second one. That had been altogether too close. She was about to lift the tray of delicate crystallised flowers when a silent shadow passed the door. Putting her eye to the crack, Lilith froze as she saw Kerr shake something over the bowl of syllabub then walk briskly away. It happened so fast she could almost have thought she'd dreamt it. Except she knew she hadn't. She emerged and gazed in perturbation at tiny flecks, just settling into the creamy froth.

'Here's the second syllabub and we're shy a footman. Johnny says he's never going to . . . ' Hester's voice tailed off in surprise at her mistress's expression.

'Don't put the bowl down,' Lilith told her urgently. 'We mustn't get them mixed up. Stay right there.' She picked up the first bowl and whirled into the kitchen. 'Catherine, you need to make a replacement for this. I don't care what — something fast and showy. I think Mr Kerr has poisoned the top. No, don't taste it! I am going to run the pump until the contents have been washed clean away. Then the bowl needs scouring thoroughly before it is used again. Come with me, Johnny, and start pumping. It will take your mind off the lilac-scented gentleman whom I don't doubt is even now being run out of the house with his tail between his legs. That's it, keep going while I wipe it around with this cloth. Very good. You may ask Cook for one of the sweet-meats and then help with the washing. There is no need to go back into the dining room.'

She dashed back into the passage where Hester was still holding the second bowl of orange syllabub. 'Thank you. Let's get these flowers scattered on it.'

Nicholas Dacre slid through the baize door, lean and deadly. 'Vale's gone,' he said. 'Where's Catherine? I saw Kerr come through here.'

'He didn't go into the kitchen. He was too busy poisoning a bowl of orange syllabub. Fortunately, it was the only dish on the table. I've washed it out but please warn Edward.'

'The devil he did!' Nicholas looked stunned and hurried back, passing Peter bearing the carcase of the green goose and beaming with triumph at the success of the dinner.

Behind Lilith, other dishes for the second course began to be deposited on the tables. The cold jugged hare, bullace cheese, roasted pheasants, apricot tart . . .

By the time Woods appeared, Catherine had whipped up an emergency burnt cream that Lilith also decorated with the flowers. She quickly repeated the warning to him.

Woods looked horrified. 'Seems to me it's a shame he ever recovered.' He picked up the hare, nodded to Peter to bring the jug of gravy and led his stately procession back.

Lilith leaned against the wall, her legs trembling, her head throbbing. She had done all she could. It was up to Edward now.

19

Ned saw the moment Sir Mortimer Vale touched his youngest footman. He was still irked with the man for arriving without an invitation and was viewing with disfavour the rate at which the level in Vale's glass was dropping. When Johnny gave a startled yelp, dropping the bottle of wine he was pouring from, and then fled the room pursued by Sir Mortimer and a second later by Woods, he was very ready to take a hand.

'My unwanted guest has outstayed his welcome,' he muttered to the Duke of Rutland. 'Excuse me.' As he spoke, he saw Kerr hurry out. He'd take long odds it wasn't to calm the situation down. Even more reason to get there.

'Vale's a disgrace to his name. Tell him I said so,' replied his grace amiably.

When Ned reached the hall, Woods had a firm grip on Sir Mortimer's arm and was steering him away from the domestic wing. Kerr was nowhere in sight.

'Thank you, Woods. Sir Mortimer is leaving. Send someone for his groom.'

'Don't be so straightlaced, Makepeace,' slurred Vale. 'You'll turn a blind eye if you want my subscription.'

Behind him, Kerr appeared through the baize door. Ned's heart thumped, hoping he had not discovered Catherine in the kitchen under the pretext of checking all was well. 'I hardly think so, Vale,' he said aloud. 'I will not have my servants molested.'

'That's rich, coming from you. I hear you're heading for the parson's mousetrap. You want to take a look at the lady's sketchbook before you start spreading slander about me. Damned if I'd go for tainted goods.'

Ned took two quick paces forward. 'Sir Mortimer's hat and gloves, Woods. You are a guest in my house, Vale, so I am unable to punish that remark as I would wish to.'

'You can't, but I can,' said Nicholas Dacre, leaning negligently against the wall by the dining room. 'It would be a pleasure. I've been looking for a new scandal to get embroiled in.'

'Don't trouble yourself,' sneered Sir Mortimer. 'I'm leaving. Inform Wellham I'll send the carriage back.' He swaggered outside.

Dacre jerked his head silently towards Kerr, held up at the door by the footmen clearing the first course. 'You get back to your guests,' he said aloud. 'I'll wait here until he goes.'

And check the kitchen for yourself as soon as Kerr's out of sight, if I don't miss my guess. Ned nodded assent and followed his secretary into the dining room. By the sideboard, Kerr paused, caught sight of Ned watching him, and moved smoothly to the corner table where the notes for the presentation were stacked. Ned's skin prickled. He was up to something, but what?

The dishes for the second course were brought in to a general murmur of appreciation. The Duke of Rutland had a twinkle in his eye as a bowl of orange syllabub was placed near him.

'Subtle, Makepeace, but appreciated.'

Dacre re-entered and bent to murmur in Ned's ear. 'Kerr has just shown his hand. He wasn't checking on the footman. Lilith saw him add something to one of the dishes in the passage. She's scoured it out and everything now on the table is safe. But Kerr isn't.'

Poison in his own house! Ned could hardly swallow for abhorrence. He recalled those times overseas when he and Ricky had been subject to digestive trouble. He remembered Kerr's efficiency in mixing them a remedy to clear it up. That medicine cabinet of his, packed with tablets and powders . . . Is that what he intended tonight? A little something to give the guests a bad stomach and ensure they didn't support his trip to Greece? A final vicious fling of the dice because Ned and Lilith had overcome all the other potential disasters designed to humiliate him?

Ned helped the Duke to a portion of the syllabub. Out of the corner of his eye he saw his secretary watching with satisfaction. Revulsion shuddered through him. Embezzlement was one thing, possibly helping Atkins to his end was another, introducing Ricky to opium quite a big step more, but causing mass harm to innocent people, purely to revenge himself on one man? That was the act of a monster. Flint or no Flint, Kerr would be out of this house tomorrow. If Dacre wanted him watched, he could damn well tail him to London himself.

Ned ate and conversed, mentally planning what to do. Thanks to Lilith, no damage had taken place and Kerr had no idea he'd been found out. He would not be expecting any action to be taken against him. They could lock all the storerooms now, warn everyone in the house to be on their guard, then Ned could dismiss Kerr in the morning, stand over him while he packed, and send him on his way.

The dishes were removed, port and brandy placed on the table and Ned stood up. Dacre sauntered out of the room to get Catherine back to Furze House before anyone else was heading off.

'Gentlemen,' said Ned. 'I regret to say this is where you pay for your supper.'

A ripple of laughter went around the room.

Ned held out his hand for Kerr to pass his speech. He didn't really need the notes. By now he could give the presentation blindfold. Even so, he fanned the pages — and saw at once that the middle sheets were out of order. It was the final stroke. He turned his head and gave his secretary a cold, contemplative stare. Then he put his speech down on the table and collected the attention of his guests. 'The ancient cities of Greece,' he began, 'have long held a fascination for us . . . '

He was told later that he'd spoken well and eloquently, but he didn't remember a single word. Carriages were called, promises were made. As he bid his guests farewell, Ned vowed that he would never, ever put himself though this again.

'Bed,' he said to his brother as the door finally closed. 'You're all in. Thank you for your support tonight.'

Ricky coloured, made as if to say something, then changed his mind. 'It was a good dinner,' he said. 'Lord, I'm tired. Goodnight.'

Lilith emerged cautiously from the kitchen wing, followed by Woods with the tea tray. 'Are you pleased?' she asked. 'Woods said if he had any money, he'd have backed you.'

'Time will tell. Lilith, that was a triumph of organisation. I cannot thank you enough.' He glanced around the entrance hall for Kerr, but there was no sign of him. Good. He was sick beyond measure of watching his words, of pretending all was well, of preserving a decorous distance from the woman he . . . yes, from the woman he loved.

'I own it is nice to be able to breathe again,' said Lilith with a faint smile as they moved into the quiet library.

Woods placed the tray on a table and withdrew, closing the door. The fire crackled. Ned gazed affectionately at this miraculous woman who had come so unexpectedly into his life and made herself at home. 'I believe even if we were in the desert, you would contrive tea for us.'

She smiled. 'One must keep up standards.'

He caught her hands. 'Would you like to visit the desert with me? Would you like to see Alexandria, or Damascus, or Athens?'

'Very much,' she whispered.

He pulled her closer, smiling down into her grey-green eyes. And saw them widen at something past his shoulder, felt her stiffen and step away. He swung around, furious at being interrupted yet again. And then abruptly became very wary indeed.

Kerr had been concealed in one of the wing chairs. On a low table next to him were two glasses of wine. He handed them one each and retreated to pour a third for himself. 'A toast to your success,' he said in his impersonal fashion. 'It went very well.'

Kerr never poured wine. He rarely sat in the library, preferring his own set of rooms. Ned cursed himself for a fool. That stare he'd given him must have raised the man's suspicions. Of all the ridiculous things to have broken through his guard.

Before he could tell Lilith not to drink, she regarded her glass thoughtfully, gave a smile of thanks and put the wine down untasted. 'That is kind, but I would prefer tea.'

'Wine is more traditional when congratulations are in order.'

Her well-shaped brows expressed surprise at the secretary's insistence.

There was too much furniture in here, thought Ned. If he tried to tackle

Kerr in a hurry, he'd break his shins before he could get to him. 'If we are talking tradition, then it should be a dram, shouldn't it?' he said, strolling forward until there was clear space between them. That was better. 'How remiss of us not to purchase whisky the other day. Tell me, Kerr, do you hate me very much?'

'I . . . ' Kerr was caught off-balance by the question. 'I am your secretary. Personal feelings are irrelevant. I wish merely to drink to your triumph.'

Ned held his wine up to the light as if admiring the colour. 'Irrelevant? Then sabotaging my dinner and my speech being out of order was accidental, was it?'

Kerr gave a faint, superior smile. 'You are imaging things.' His eyes went from Ned to Lilith. 'But then, there has been a lot on your mind.'

Ned felt his patience snap. 'I didn't *imagine* meeting your supposed former employer Mr Highside at Cheveley last week,' he said. 'It was strange that he had never heard of you. Nor did I *imagine* your family being listed amongst those affected by my father's clearance of the Scottish estate. That *would* be a legitimate grievance on your part, but it was my father's decision, and his alone. It has always been my opinion that the tenants were unfairly treated. Try as I might, I cannot see why you should hate me personally.'

That Kerr had never expected to be unmasked was evident. Shocked and angry, he shed all vestiges of humanity. 'Your family are thieves,' he said, his eyes glittering. 'There can be no distinction between you. The sins of the father shall be visited on the children. I proposed a toast, Miss Fitzgilbert. Drink please.' In his other hand he suddenly, preposterously, held a small pistol. It was pointing directly at Lilith.

* * *

Lilith froze into stillness, unable to look away from the deadly silver muzzle. The thought crossed her mind that people who blithely claimed danger to be stimulating, grossly exaggerated the matter.

'Put it down,' said Edward in a level voice. 'One shot and I promise you'll be dead before you draw your next breath.'

'As will Miss Fitzgilbert,' replied Kerr. 'You will suffer her loss for the rest of your life, just as my mother suffered when my father died. Have you ever been to the east coast of Scotland? The wind is merciless and the ground is barren. A more God-forsaken place doesn't exist. It broke my father. All so *your* father's bank vault could grow fat with bloodied gold.'

'Is that why you've been robbing me?'

Fury crossed Kerr's face. 'No, *that* was to pay off Flint, damn him. But it was so simple, it seemed a shame not to carry on. Who told you? Not Atkins. He had too much to lose on his own account.'

'We found the wage lists,' replied

Edward. Lilith noticed he'd edged forward another half step. 'Yours, and the one Mrs Gunn left behind. The differences were startling. Who is Flint?'

'The devil incarnate. You are not drinking, Miss Fitzgilbert. Please do. I would prefer not to use the pistol. I dislike violence.'

For a near-hysterical moment, Lilith wondered why she should be expected to make things more agreeable for a man who was trying to kill her. 'What is in the wine?' she asked.

His gaze rested on her. 'It will not help you to know. I regret to inform you some of the guests will experience cramps tonight. You will be thought to have eaten more of whatever caused them. I had not planned it this way, but it will serve very well. I assure you the wine will not be unpleasant. That in itself is more than you deserve, having thwarted my plans, alerted Mr Makepeace to my revenge *and* forced me to take opium.' His voice hardened. 'I will never forgive you for that.'

'You were the one screaming with pain,' said Lilith. 'If you had not increased the dosage in Mr Richard's bottle, the laudanum would have done you no harm.'

'It was interference. You are constantly interfering. I was in control until you arrived. He didn't notice a thing. But *you* installed your own footman. *You* replaced the cook. *You* read Mrs Makepeace's letter, meaning we had to come here early and miss them.'

'Good God,' said Edward. 'What were you planning to do to Henry and Leonora?'

'They were going to bring the *children*,' hissed Kerr, his face contorted.

Lilith's blood ran cold. A glance at Edward's face showed him pale with horror. 'What hold did Flint have on you?' he managed.

Kerr sneered contemptuously. 'Well, why shouldn't I say? Why shouldn't I tell you that a man from a family you deemed worthless is cleverer than all of you? I joined your household as the easiest way to get to your father.'

'My father?' Edward clearly hadn't expected that. 'But I rarely saw him. The only time I went to Hampshire was at Christmas, and you always travelled to Scotland then.'

'Naturally I could not go to Hampshire. His steward would have known my name. The steward, however, didn't go to Lord Hare's house party.'

Lilith caught her breath. The house party where Edward had been supposed to offer for Lady Isabel. The one where his father had had a seizure while waiting for the hunt to start. The one where he had died.

Kerr was still talking, his voice high, gloating in his own cleverness. 'One footman looks much like another to those with their noses in the air. It was a shame he had to die so fast. He didn't suffer as my father suffered.'

The toast to the hunt. The traditional drink before the riders set off. One footman looks much like another . . . 'Oh, of course,' said Lilith, 'you were an apothecary. You put something in his glass of port at the beginning of the meet. That was very clever.' Without conscious thought she added the hint of interested admiration in her tone that went down so well with her stepmother's artistic protégés. Perhaps if they kept him talking, his grip on that pistol would loosen.

'No one even suspected, or so I thought. I was shocked when I received the letter from Flint demanding money. He had been present. He saw me. He wanted a single sum to wipe out the secret. For a while I was very angry with him.' Kerr's smile made Lilith shiver. 'But it's an ill wind that blows no one any good. The house where I took the payment showed me another way to revenge myself on your family. An interesting place, Wardour Street.'

Lilith saw Edward's fingers whiten on the stem of his glass. 'And Atkins?' he asked.

'That lazy, vainglorious fool! I didn't mind him running things down — the more uncomfortable you were, the better I was pleased. But then he threatened to tell you I had dismissed Mrs Gunn. He wanted me to buy his silence. I wasn't having that. White arsenic in a nip of brandy to seal the deal and a trip to the ditch by moonlight. It was as easy as tickling a trout.'

He was inhuman. A cold-blooded, two-times murderer. And he still had the pistol trained on her. But . . . but once he had fired, Edward would be able to overcome him and be safe. And then Benedict could investigate that list of possible names for Flint. Lilith took a slow breath. It was up to her. She wondered with detached interest whether the cushioned back of the nearest winged chair would be sufficient to shield her from the bullet or would merely slow it down?

'That explains why his valises were dry,' said Edward. 'You needed time to pack them. Did you think I wouldn't notice?'

Kerr's eyes were full of scorn. 'You?

You are too involved in your work to be observant. It's her fault. She's ruined all my plans.' His voice grew thick with hatred. 'You weren't supposed to die yet. Not until your brother comes of age. I can manage him easily. I managed you until she came. Jezebel, never eating here, planting her spies, blinding you with lust.' He swung back to Lilith, raising the pistol. 'You with your unnatural learning and your serpent wits, finding me out and making him ever more of a fool. I *belong* here, the income is mine by *right*, and now I have to go. This is all due to you.'

Lilith was appalled. The malice spewing out of him was like a spear thrust. She felt pinned by it, unable to move. She had to. She would throw herself behind the chair. It was time. *Be lucky, Edward.*

But Edward was not pinned by the malice. The moment Kerr's attention was off him, he shouted 'Down!' and dashed his glass of wine in the man's face. Lilith dropped to the floor like a stone as the pistol jerked and fired over her head.

The door burst open. Woods and Peter crowded in. Edward leapt to grapple murderously with his former secretary. With madness in his eyes, Kerr lunged for Lilith's forgotten wine and drank it down in one.

20

'Lilith?'

Lilith quickly rose from where she had been sitting by the fire in her room. 'Edward,' she said, letting her sketch-book fall to the floor. 'Is it . . . has he . . . ?'

His arms came around her, safe and strong, blessedly normal. Behind him, she saw Hester slip away.

'The coroner has just left,' said Edward. 'Kerr's body has been taken to the Three Blackbirds ready for the inquest. You and I must attend, but the coroner is satisfied with our evidence. It is enough that Kerr hated my family, that his blind entitlement ate away at his reason. There will be no need to bring his dealings with Flint into it. I don't suppose your brother wishes that complication bandied abroad just yet.'

'No.' She rested her head against his

shoulder. Another moment and she would have enough courage to say what still must be cleared up between them.

'We will forget all this, and we shall be happy. Dearest Lilith, will you . . . ?'

She lifted her head. 'Wait.'

'I will not wait. I have been interrupted too many times already. If I do not say this now, your maid will come back with hot milk for you, or Woods will tell us the youngest footman has run away or . . . '

Lilith laid a finger very gently on his lips. That in itself, knowing she had the power to still his words, was a sensation quite as intense as the feeling of his arms around her, claiming her, guarding her against the world. 'Edward, I must say this. There must be no secrets between us. Woods told me Sir Mortimer mentioned my sketchbook and advised you to look at it.'

'I have seen your sketchbook. You draw divinely. You do everything divinely. Lilith, please will you . . . ?'

She stepped back and picked the

book up. 'This is why,' she said, handing it to him. Now he would know her for a rebel, for an indelicate female who could jeopardise his future contacts and career. She would not cry, she told herself. She would not.

He studied the page she had turned to. 'A reclining male figure, nicely delineated. Why is this a problem?'

'Edward, I disguised myself as a male student to go to Sir Thomas Lawrence's life-drawing lecture.'

He closed the book and skimmed it on to the chair. 'Outmoded Royal Academy rules. I said as much to Thornley when he told me of the uproar.'

Lilith felt her face break into a smile as she melted against him. 'Dearest Edward, I do love you.'

He held her even more tightly. 'And I love you, Lilith, very much. Nothing you say or do will ever scandalise me or prevent me from adoring you, though I hope you will agree after careful study that my muscles are superior to those of Lawrence's model.'

She tipped up her face to his, her smile growing. 'You will let me sketch you?'

'It will be my wedding present to you.'

'Riches. The only gift to match it is to bring Woods with me as our butler.'

Her paramour contrived to look noble. 'I promise your possession of Woods did not weigh with me *at all* on reaching my decision to offer for you. Will you be my wife, Lilith?'

'Yes, Edward.'

'Even though I have so many bad character traits I can barely enumerate them?'

'Yes, for I have not noticed any at all.'

'I must warn you we are likely to always have Ricky with us.'

'No, we won't. He is going to ask you tomorrow about entering Cambridge.'

'In that case, I must tell you that, according to Kerr, I cannot afford to marry.'

'I do not altogether trust his judgement on that, but fortunately I have enough for both of us.'

Edward was startled enough to loosen his hold on her. 'Really?'

And that was another reason she loved him.

'Dearest Edward, you have met Benedict. Does it seem conceivable to you that his only sister should *not* have money?'

'Do you mean to tell me, you impossible woman, that all the time I was struggling to raise funds for my Greek expedition, you could have underwritten it on your own?'

'Well, not to the extent that it would beggar me,' temporised Lilith. 'I might require rather more in the way of comfort and fashion on a daily basis than you deem necessary, for example.'

'Then why did you make me go through with that ghastly dinner?'

'It wasn't ghastly. It was a triumph. Even Kerr said so.'

'We have already agreed his judgment is faulty.'

She smiled lovingly at him, the one

man in the world who desired her for her mind alone. 'Think, Edward, if I had told you the extent of my fortune, how would I have known if it was me you wanted or my funds? None of my previous suitors have ever been able to make the distinction.'

He gazed at her, incensed. 'Call yourself intelligent? This is how you'd know. Or you would have done, had I ever been allowed to finish a proposal of marriage.'

Before Lilith could utter another word he bent his mouth to hers and proceeded to kiss her in a thoroughly enlightening fashion.

'Now do you understand?' he murmured, some time later.

Lilith ran a tongue experimentally over her lips. She felt warm, and secure, and deeply loved. 'I'm not sure,' she said. 'I think you had better show me again.'

Acknowledgements

Any mistakes are my own,
but I owe particular thanks to

Louise Allen, for unstintingly sharing
all her detailed Regency knowledge
https://www.louiseallenregency.co.uk/

Newmarket Local History Group
for all the work that has gone into
collating photos, plans and articles
about Newmarket through the ages

Kate Johnson for so much
support, always

My friends, both online and offline,
for simply being there

and you, if I've forgotten to
include you

SURFING INTO DANGER

Ken Preston

All Eden wants to do is roam the coast surfing, at one with the waves and her board, winning enough in competitions to finance her nomadic lifestyle. But first the mysterious Finn, and then a disastrous leak from a recycling plant, scupper her plans. With surfing out of the question, Eden investigates. As the crisis deepens, who can she trust — and will she and her friends make it out alive from Max Charon's sinister plastics plant?

HIS DAUGHTER'S DUTY

Wendy Kremer

Upon her father's death, Lucinda Harting learns that she faces an impoverished future unless she agrees to marry Lord Laurence Ellesporte, who reveals that his father and hers had made the arrangement in order to amalgamate the two estates. For her sake and that of the servants, she accepts, though they live mostly separate lives. Until one day when shocking news reaches Lucinda's ears: Laurence has been arrested as a spy in France! Determined to secure his release, she heads to Rouen with Laurence's aunt Eliza, and a bold plan . . .

SUMMER OF WEDDINGS

Sarah Purdue

Claire loves her job as a teacher, but always looks forward to the long summer break when she can head out into the world in search of new adventures. However, this summer is different. This summer is full of weddings. When Claire meets Gabe, a handsome American in a black leather jacket and motorbike boots, on the way to her best friend Lorna's do, she wonders if this will be her most adventurous summer yet. Will the relationship end in heartache, or a whole new world of possibilities?

LOVE CHILD

Penny Oates

Knowing she was adopted, Lara was nevertheless happy with the parents who brought her up. But when she accidentally discovers her birth parents, she is catapulted into a life completely alien to her — and comes up against the insurmountable obstacle that is Dominic Leigh. She can't understand why he seems determined to keep her away from her father, or why he suspects her of wanting to cause trouble. She vows to overcome his interference, and in doing so, finds so much more than she had bargained for . . .